"The Executioner is, despite all the bloodshed, one of the better-written series of its type. It is the biggie of the genre."

—*The Washington Star*

Yes, here it is—the book that became a best-selling series and changed the image of the American hero. Mack Bolan is the Executioner, a self-appointed one-man army fighting an endless battle against organized crime. He's ruthless . . . he's savage . . . he's the hard, cold, uncompromising warrior of the seventies!

This is a work of fiction. All the characters and events portrayed in this book are fictional, and any resemblance to real people or incidents is purely coincidental.

THE EXECUTIONER: WAR AGAINST THE MAFIA

An original Pinnacle Books edition, published for the first time anywhere.

ISBN: 0-523-40299-6

First printing, March 1969
Second printing, September 1969
Third printing, April 1970
Fourth printing, October 1970
Fifth printing, December 1970
Sixth printing, June 1971
Seventh printing, December 1971
Eighth printing, June 1972
Ninth printing, July 1972
Tenth printing, November 1972
Eleventh printing, January 1974
Twelfth printing, March 1974
Thirteenth printing, December 1974
Fourteenth printing, May 1975
Fifteenth printing, September 1975
Sixteenth printing, August 1976
Seventeenth printing, April 1978

Cover illustration by Gil Cohen

Printed in the United States of America

PINNACLE BOOKS, INC.
One Century Plaza
2029 Century Park East
Los Angeles, California 90067

An introduction to the new edition of
War Against the Mafia

I am presently finalizing the 27th segment of the Executioner saga—which means that I have produced, to date, something on the order of 5,000 book pages on the life and times of one Mack Bolan. That's a pretty hefty biography—eight years in the writing and only God knows how many more ahead.

It should be simple, then, shouldn't it, to turn out a two or three page introduction for a special re-issue of the first book in that series, to offer some special insight from the author's point of view.

Wrong.

I cannot find an objectivity to serve the purpose.

And certainly I cannot say in three pages what I have been struggling to impart throughout the past five thousand. I have been trying to say—through Bolan's viewpoint and from the very beginning—something particularly important and urgent about the human situation. It is there, somewhere, (that statement) in each of the books—and yet it is not *wholly* there in any of the books nor in any combination, not in any recognizable message form—primarily, I guess, because I am not really sure, myself, just what that message is. I'm still working on it. If I ever do manage to capture the full meaning of Bolan's situation then that will probably be the end of the series—the story will have been told. Perhaps then I can go back and write some sort of dazzlingly introspectful introduction. At the moment, I cannot do that. I am as much in awe of Bolan and his story as is any of the faithful fans who keep my correspondence desk littered with their written reactions to this modern day Quixote.

A writer's first obligation is to entertain his readers, whatever the fictional format. I have tried to do that as the first order of business. I have attempted to match the prose to the man, to tailor each story to its setting, and to keep faith with the basic character of the hero. That may sound much easier than it actually is. Writing is a continual process of problem-solving, groping with ideas and trying to fit words into them, developing characters and plotline, establishing theme and conflict, keeping the whole thing together and moving line by line down the pages in such a way that the reader will be drawn into the process and become a sentient part of it. The writer himself must of course be part of that process; indeed, he must be at the very center of it. He must, himself, be entertained by the story he is weaving, feel involved in it. It's a very emotional business. If

I cannot feel—then Bolan also cannot. If I cannot care enough to know anger, or outrage, or sympathy, or compassion—can I ask more of my characters? Can I ask my readers to be moved or even entertained if I myself am above all that?

No, obviously, I cannot.

My "style" of writing, then, is an attempt to entertain myself. It is a movement toward self-involvement, an empathetic participation, in the affairs of Mack Bolan. Being a rather average guy, myself, I then assume that what involves me will also involve my readers. When I laugh, I assume that they are laughing with me—not at me. And when I weep . . . yeah.

So, no, I cannot be objective in any personal look at the Bolan stories. They have constituted my very life for these past eight years. I have not become Mack Bolan—and Bolan has not become me—but I would hate to have to be the one to go in and attempt to sort out the pieces of personality that have become intertwined during that eight-year association, to determine which is me and which is Bolan. As I have grown as a writer, Bolan has grown as a character. And with each forward step of the character, the challenge to the author grows in direct proportion.

Andy Ettinger, who has been my editor through most of these years, kindly offered me an opportunity to make whatever revisions I should like to make in the original story for this special re-issue. And there are various things that I would handle a bit differently, no doubt, if I were just now undertaking this book for the first time. But I really do not wish to change anything. This original presentation of Mack Bolan is the raw stuff from which the man and his war has been fashioned, and it would not be right to now go back and rearrange the events or the circumstances attending his birth. He is not the same man today as he was then, of course—nor am I. We have grown together and prospered together—all to the best, I hope. Whatever we may be now is a direct result of what we were, then. We will not attempt to rewrite the past. We *will* continue the attempt to entertain each other, to challenge each other, to inspire each other. And we very humbly hope that our readers will continue to share our delight with the process.

For those of you who are here for the first time: welcome, and we hope that you will become involved to the point of returning from time to time . . .

For those who have circled back for a second look at the birthing: we haven't really changed all that much, none of us—have we?

—Don Pendleton
April, 1976

PROLOGUE

Mack Bolan was not born to kill, as many of his comrades and superiors secretly believed. He was not a mechanically functioning killer-robot, as his sniper-team partners openly proclaimed. He was not even a cold-blooded and ruthless exterminator, as one leftist news correspondent tagged him. Mack was simply a man who could command himself. He was the personification of that ideal advanced by the army psychologist who screened and evaluated sniper-team candidates: "A good sniper has to be a man who can kill methodically, unemotionally, and *personally*. *Personally* because it's an entirely different ball game when you can see even the color of your victim's eyes through the magnification of a sniper-scope, when you can see the look of surprise and fear when he realizes he's been shot. Most any good soldier can be a successful sniper *once*—it's the second or third time around, when the memories of personal killing are edged into the conscience, that the 'soldiers' are separated from the 'executioners.' Killing in this manner is closely akin to murder in the conscience of many men. Of course, we do not want mad dogs in this program, either. What we want, quite simply, is a man who can distinguish between murder and duty, and who can realize that a duty killing is not an act of murder. A man who is also cool and calm when he himself is in jeopardy completes the picture of our sniper ideal."

Sergeant Mack Bolan was obviously such a man. A weapons specialist and skilled armorer, he also held marksman awards in every personal-weapon category. The sarge did not keep a personal record of his "kills," but the official accounting shows a verified total of 32 high-ranking officers of the North Vietnamese Regulars, including General Ngo An; 46 Viet Cong guerrilla leaders, and 17 VC village officials. This account of a typical sniping mission was recorded in a report filed by Sergeant Bolan's spotter, Corporal T. L. Minnegas, covering their final mission together:

> Team arrived vicinity of Station B at 0435 hours. Pvt. Thomas and Pvt. Yancey reconned and reported back "all-clear" at 0450 hours. Station B manned at 0500 hours and equipment set up. At 0630 hours village began to stir. VC recon party arrived at 0642 and checked out the village. At 0650 Tra Huong and escort arrived outside chief's house. Chief and unknown male came out to greet Huong party. Targets confirmed with Sgt. Bolan and RVNM guide. Sgt. Bolan's first round got Tra Huong (through the neck). Round two was through right temple of village chief, round three through back of Col. Huong's aide (unidentified). Departed Station B at approx. 0652 hours, all objectives accomplished. Arrived Base Camp at 0940 hours. No casualties Sniper Team Able.

Vietnam represented a new type of warfare for the American soldier. Many grim "specialties" were developed there by American youth. And perhaps none more grim nor more specialized than the one personified in Sergeant Mack Bolan. Bolan had been a career soldier. At age 30 he was a 12-year veteran and on his second Vietnam tour. He had never married. His mother, Elsa, a youthful 47-year-old second-generation Polish-American, wrote him faithfully on Tuesdays and Fridays of each week and sent him a "care" package twice monthly, each one filled with tangy Polish sausages, cookies, and a small cake or two. Her letters were always cheerful and uncomplaining, and she often enclosed snapshots of

Cindy, Mack's pretty 17-year-old sister, and of Johnny, the kid brother just turned 14. Sam Bolan, Mack's father, had been a steelworker since the age of 16. Mack always thought of Sam Bolan as being as dependable and as indestructible as the steel he made, and though Mack and Sam never corresponded directly, the letters between mother and son bore frequent messages between the Bolan men.

From one of Elsa's letters, for example: "Pop wants to know if it's true what they say about Asian women. Ha!"

And the reply from Mack: "Tell Pop there are a lot of truths about Asian women and I'm diligently seeking the full story. A-ha!"

Cindy Bolan, at the time of the tragedy, had only recently graduated from high school. Her big brother represented her ideal of masculine perfection. She wrote him each night, continuing the letter diary-fashion and mailing it weekly, often confiding her secret fears and problems in the rambling letters. Example: "Mary Ann keeps trying to talk me into going to a pot party with her. Have you ever smoked pot? I hear it is used widely over there."

Counselor Mack's reply from across the sea was: "With friends like Mary Ann, you don't have much need of enemies, do you. As for myself, I have plenty enemies enough over here without adding pot to the list."

In another exchange, Cindy remarked: "It's always a problem. I mean, you know, how much is *too* much? I never had that problem with Steve, but Chuck keeps me shook up all the time. I mean, he has a *hands* problem. Know what I mean? I'm crazy about him but I don't know just how to handle this problem of his."

The responding counsel from her brother was typical. "Chuck doesn't have the problem, honey," he wrote. "*You* have it. You know how to handle it if you really want to handle it. Right?"

Cindy's reply to that also typified these personal exchanges between brother and sister: "Oh, by the way, no more Chuck problem. How did I handle it? *No more Chuck!!!*"

In a letter from Mrs. Bolan dated in late spring, she told her son: "Now that the worst is past I suppose I should tell you that Pop has been having a bit of a rough time. He had a light heart attack in January, and the doctor would not let him work for a while. We pinched pennies and got through okay on the sickness benefits and Pop is back to work now and everything looks bright. Of course a few bills piled up but we'll catch up okay. Cindy had already decided to work a year before starting college, and I guess that's what bothered Pop the most—Cindy's education. He has always felt bad about not seeing you through college, you know. But—all is well now so there's nothing for you to worry about. And you are *not* to send any money home. Pop would have a *fit!*"

On the following August 12th, Sergeant Bolan was summoned to his base camp chaplain's office, where he learned of his father's death. And of his mother's. And of his sister's. The official communiqué also advised that young Johnny Bolan was in critical condition but was expected to survive. Bolan was air-lifted home on emergency leave to handle funeral arrangements and to see to the care of his orphaned brother.

It was a sad and traumatic home-coming for this professional soldier. The trauma was deepened when Sergeant Bolan learned the circumstances of the deaths from the homicide detective who met him at the airport. The elder Bolan had evidently "gone berserk" and, without apparent provocation, had shot his wife, son, and daughter, finally turning the gun on himself. Only the son survived.

It was another 48 hours before young Johnny Bolan was removed from the hospital's critical list and the grieving soldier could fully piece together the events leading to the tragedy. Johnny's statement to a police stenographer, delivered from a hospital bed, reads as follows:

> Pop had been sick and couldn't work for a while. He got behind in some bills and he was worried about some money he borrowed about a year ago. Then he went back to work and he could not do the job he had been doing, because of his heart, and the job they gave him did not pay as much. He was worried about that, because of the bills and being behind, and then these guys were starting to bother him at work. These guys he owed some money to. I heard him tell Mama one night that they were blood-suckers, that they didn't even want to leave him enough every week to take care of his family. He said they could all go to hell. Then one night he came home with his arm pulled out of the socket. His shoulder, I mean. These goons had worked him over. Mama got all tore up over that. She was scared he would have another heart attack. She was going to call the cops but Pop wouldn't let her. He said they'd just start taking it out on her and the kids. I heard Mama telling Cindy about it. Then things got okay again, a few weeks ago. Pop couldn't understand, but he was telling Mama these goons had been leaving him alone, and he sure wasn't going to go ask them why. Then the other night something happened. I don't know what. I just know Pop started yelling and blowing his stack. Mama and Cindy were trying to quiet him down, they were afraid he'd have another attack. Then next thing I knew he had this old gun of his and he was blasting away with it. One of the shots got me. Then Pop went back in his bedroom and I heard one more shot just before I passed out. That's all I know.

It was "all" Johnny knew for the official police record, and the statement was sufficient to close the case as "murder-suicide." For Sergeant Mack Bolan, however, the case was anything but closed. Johnny had no desire to withhold anything from his brother, and in a private conversation with Mack, he confided that Cindy had become involved with the "goons" who had been pressuring their father.

"She went to see these guys," Johnny said, "and told them about Pop's heart and asked them to lay off'f him. She told me about that. What she didn't tell me was about this later deal she let them talk her into. At first she was just turning her paycheck over to them every week. She was only getting thirty-five a week, and that was supposed to be going in the bank for her college, you know. Then I found out what she'd started doing for them. She started working for those guys, Mack. She was—sellin' her ass. Don't look at me like that, she *was*. I followed her one night and I found out for myself. I knew something was bothering her. I wasn't trying to spy on her, I just wanted to know what was wrong. Well, I caught her. I followed her to this motel, and I hung around outside. I saw this guy go in. After he left, I busted in. The door wasn't even locked. Cindy was on the bed, bare-assed and crying. She about died when she saw me. She said she had to get that money paid back quick, or they'd go to work on Pop again. She said they gave her a month, just one month, to cough up five hundred bucks, and they told her how she could earn the money. They set the whole thing up, and sent this guy she called Leo around to talk to her. Leo set up dates for her. He'd call her and tell her the time and the place. She had just finished her third 'date' when I caught her. I told her it was no good, that Pop wouldn't want it that way. She said it wasn't a matter of what Pop wanted or didn't want, it was just a matter of what had to be done. Well, I couldn't get anywhere with her.

So I did a dumb thing. All I could think of was telling Pop. I knew he'd straighten Cindy out. I mean, I knew he wouldn't hold still for what she was doing. God, Mack, I didn't think he'd go nuts. And he did. He went completely ape. Right off the bat he busted me in the mouth. Knocked me flat. I saw stars. I was layin' there on the floor and he was yelling and jumping around like something gone crazy. You know what I think? I think he must've had some idea that something funny had been going on. I mean, the look in his eyes when I told him. Like the light dawning, you know. Just the same, I never saw him like that before. He reached down and got ahold of me again and he was slapping me with his open hand and yelling, "Tell me you're lying, tell me you're lying!"

"Then Cindy came running in. She was trying to pull Pop offa me, and both of them were yelling and screaming. Pop let go of me finally and I don't really know what they were saying to each other, except Pop kept muttering, 'It's a lie, it's a lie'—and Cindy was trying to explain that it didn't matter, that it wasn't that important. Oh yeah—she told him she'd sell her soul if that's what it took, that he meant more to her than any lousy phoney morality—and I think that's what really touched him off. He got real quiet then, and then Mama came running in. That's how fast all this happened. Mama had been in the bedroom asleep, and you know how light she sleeps. By the time she got awake and could get in there, all the shouting had ended.

"She and Cindy started trying to fix my mouth, trying to stop the bleeding. Pop was standing in a corner, his arms folded across his chest, and he was just looking at us. I don't think I'll ever forget the look on his face, Mack. I remember he said something silly, real silly, in that quiet way he had of talking sometimes, you remember? The sort of meditating voice? He said, 'Cindy, I want you to get an education, honey.' I don't think

Cindy heard him. She was trying to get some ice out of a tray, to put on my lip, I guess. Anyhow she didn't say anything back to him. He walked out of the room, back toward his bedroom. Next thing I knew, Pop was back, standing in the doorway. He had that old pistol in his hand, that old Smith and Wesson Uncle Billy gave him. I tried to yell something, but I didn't get a chance. Mama and Cindy were both mother-henning me, hovering over me. He shot *me* first. I actually saw him pull the trigger, I mean I saw his finger moving. Then it was like the world coming to an end. He just kept on pulling that trigger. I saw Mama and Cindy go down and still he kept shooting. He stood there staring at me after the gun was empty, just staring at *me*. Mama and Cindy were laying across me and one of Mama's arms was on my head. I was peeping at him around Mama's body. It was like he didn't even know Mama and Cindy were there, like it was just me'n him. He looked me right in the eye and said, 'I'm sorry I busted your lip, John-O.' Then he just turned around and went back out, back toward the bedroom. Coupla minutes later I heard another shot. Then somebody started banging on the front door and I passed out."

Mack Bolan's only comment to his brother's emotional story was a hushed, "Son of a bitch." This entry from the diary, however, dated August 16th, is more revelatory of his reaction to the triple tragedy:

"Cindy did only what she thought had to be done. In his own mixed-up way, I guess Pop did the same. Can I do any less?"

And on August 17th, Bolan wrote: "It looks like I have been fighting the wrong enemy. Why defend a front line 8,000 miles away when the *real* enemy is chewing up everything you love back home? I have talked to the police about this situation and they seem to be helpless to do anything. The problem, as I see it, is that the rules of warfare are all rigged against the cops.

Just *knowing* the enemy isn't enough. They have to *prove* he's the enemy, and even then sometimes he slips away from them. What is needed here is a bit of direct action, strategically planned, and to hell with the rules. Over in 'Nam we called it a 'war of attrition.' Seek out and destroy. Exterminate the enemy. I guess it's time a war was declared on the home front. The same kind of war we've been fighting at 'Nam. The very same kind."

On August 18th a sportsman's shop in Pittsfield was burglarized. The owner reported that a high-powered hunting rifle, a deluxe scope, some targets, and several boxes of ammunition had been taken. An envelope of money sufficient to cover the loss had been left on the cash register. "It was just a midnight sale with no salesman present," the shopkeeper told police. "Evidently nothing else was disturbed and, from my standpoint, no crime has been committed."

On August 19th the watchman at a deserted stone quarry several miles from Pittsfield investigated the sounds of gunfire in one of the back canyons of the quarry. "I didn't go all the way down in there to talk to the guy," the watchman later reported. "He wasn't hurting anything or anybody. He'd set up this target range and he was plunkin' shots into the target from about a hundred yards out. Some sort of high-power rifle, sounded stronger'n a .30-06 but you know those rock walls build up sound, so I couldn't really say. I watched him for a little while. It looked like he was doing something to the gun every now'n then, you know, adjusting it or something. He'd fire five rounds, then fiddle with the gun, five more rounds, then fiddle some more. Must've been out there a couple hours, but I didn't go down in there to say anything to him. It's a perfect place for target practice. He wasn't hurting nothing. I get in some pistol practice around here myself. What's there to hurt?"

Another entry from Bolan's diary, dated August 19th, reads:

"The Marlin really surprised me I had never used a .444 before. I'd guess the muzzle energy at about a ton and a half. Enough there, anyhow, to bring down a grizzly. I should not have any trouble with the *rats* I have in mind. I sighted it in at a hundred, a hundred and ten, and a hundred and twenty yards, and the corrections are calibrated onto the scope. No sweat. I softened the lever action some, little too much tension there for the rapid-fire I need. I am going up to the drop tomorrow and verify the range, though, using the scope. I want no error."

On August 21st, Bolan wrote:

"Okay, I have located and identified the first bunch and I am ready. The police lieutenant told me all about TIF. That is Triangle Industrial Finance. They're a licensed loan outfit okay, but they use loan shark tactics and they've found a way to gimmick the law and get their rates up sky-high. The law can't touch them—but *The Executioner* can. My recon is complete and target identification is positive. Laurenti is the wheel, the OIC of the local setup. Every night at 1750 hours his car is parked at the curb in front by the man called *Mister* Erwin. The other *Mister* is a troop called Janus—*Mister* Janus. Must be some kind of a joke. The only ones they call 'Mister' are the ones with side-arms. They wear them in shoulder holsters. The one who looks like a salesman is named Brokaw. I believe he runs the office details. The college-boy type is Pete Rodriguez. He's an accountant, and as big a louse as any of them. The five of them leave the office at 1800 hours every night, give or take a minute or two, and go out to their substations to pick up collections from their legmen. Later they make personal calls on slow accounts. But not tomorrow night! The Executioner has a little collection substation of his own all set up, on the fourth floor of the Delsey building. It's a perfect drop. I ran my triangulations last night and again tonight. It will be like picking rats out of a barrel. The setup sort of reminds me of the site at Nha Tran. The targets will not have any place to go but *down*—to the ground. And that's just where I want them. I'll take the two 'Misters' first. That will plug the possibility of return fire and cut down on wild lead flying around. No problems I can see. I will have plenty of time for Laurenti. I timed out at six seconds on the dry run tonight and that was figuring them to scatter in all directions after the first round. I think I will better that time tomorrow because I do not believe these troops have been under fire before. I will probably be half done before the reaction even begins. Well, we will see. We will see, Pop."

On August 22nd, eight days following the interment of Boland's dead relatives, five officials of a loan company were gunned down on the street outsido the company office in Pittsfield, Bolan's home town. The following is an account of the incident by an eyewitness, a news vendor whose stand is located on the corner near where the shooting occurred:

"These five guys come outta the loan company. It's about closing time. Two is kinda arguing about something. One is carrying this satchel. They're standing beside this car, parked there at the curb in front of the office. One walks out inna street. Going around to the driver's side, I guess. Then he stops right in his tracks and kinda jerks around. His head snaps back toward me. I see his eyes, he's that close, and they're wide and surprised. I see blood spurting outta his neck. I see all this before I even hear the first shot. It comes from up high, up the street some place. It booms, sort of rolls down between the buildings, you know, like a echo, like a big elephant gun or something. I can't tell where it came from, not exactly, just some place up the street. It's all happening so fast. I mean, faster'n I can tell it. These guys on the sidewalk are standing there, just froze and gawking at this guy while he falls in the street. Then another one, his hands jerk up to his head just as his head starts flying off in all directions. My God, it just explodes, and I can see pieces flying every which way. The other guys are starting to scramble. One dives for the car. The other two are trying to get back inside the building. And these shots just keep rolling off, like a string of firecrackers, that fast, I mean just bing bing bing, like that. Only there's five bings. I've thought real careful about that, I know there was just five shots, like a rhythm, pow pow pow pow pow, see, just like that. And there's five dead guys strewn about there, and I mean just dead as hell. They all got it some place above the shoulders, every one of them. Gory, man, *gory.*"

A plainclothes policeman, in an off-the-record remark to a newsman, said of the kilings, "I just can't get very excited about a gang killing. And, of course, that's what this is. We've known for a long time that this outfit (the loan company) had ties with the Mafia. We just never could get anything to take into court. As long as they keep it this clean, I mean with no innocent bystanders being involved, they can knock each other off all they want to and you'll see damn few tears in *my* eyes. Yeah, it's just the underworld purging itself. It smells like gang war to me."

The officer was correct in one respect—but quite wrong in another. The attack did indeed signal the beginning of a war, but one side was strictly a one-man campaign. Duty-killer Mack Bolan had found a new battleground for an age-old cause, and had declared unconditional war on the best-organized crime syndicate in the history of the world. Note this brief entry in Bolan's diary, dated August 22nd:

"Scratch five. Results positive. Identification confirmed

by unofficial police report. *The Mafia*, for God's sake. So what? They can't be any more dangerous or any smarter than the Cong. Scratch five, and how many are left? A hundred? A thousand? Ten thousand? So—I've got another unwinnable war on my hands. So it isn't the winning that counts. It's the fighting it that goes down in the big book. The big book will say that Mack Bolan fought the good fight. That's the only kind that counts. Now to find Leo."

Executioner Bolan was taking on The Mafia.

BOOK ONE:

1—The Smiling Fates

The gold lettering on the frosted glass door read: "Plasky Enterprises." A tall man in a military uniform paused momentarily with one hand on the door, then pushed on inside and closed the door softly behind him. It was a large office, divided into small pens by a network of wrought-iron railings. Each "pen" contained a modern desk and a small table set at a right angle to the desk. Two simply upholstered metal chairs were stationed at each table. At the moment, each of the pen-style offices was vacant.

A pretty brunette occupied a reception desk outside the network of wrought iron. She was doodling on a scratch pad, the secretarial chair swivelled so that it faced the front door, her body twisted at the waist with the upper torso leaning over the desk, a silken expanse of long legs crossed at the knees and attractively displayed from a tight-fitting skirt that reached only to about midthigh. She looked up with a bored smile, not bothering to rearrange her position at the desk.

"Good morning," the visitor said. The voice was deeply pleasant and suggestive of an accustomed authority.

"Everybody's out," the girl told him, flashing her eyes toward the empty desks as though to confirm the truth of her statement ". . . if you'd like to wait . . ."

He showed frank interest in her legs, from the hem of the skirt on down, and said, "I'm Mack Bolan. Mr. Plasky said he'd see me at nine." He glanced at his watch. "It's nine now."

"Oh, well, I think maybe Mr. *Plasky* is in," the girl

said, gazing at the visitor with a newfound respect. She picked up a telephone and punched a button at the base of the instrument, all the while viewing Bolan with cool appraisal. "There's a Mr. Bolan here," she whispered into the mouthpiece; then, still holding the receiver to an ear, told Bolan: "Go on in."

The tall man angled a glance toward a door at the far end of the room and raised his eyebrows quizzically. The girl merely nodded, then giggled into the mouthpiece of the telephone and gasped, "Oh, Mr. *Plasky!*"

Bolan grinned as he pushed through a swinging gate in the wrought iron. He walked past the row of officepens and opened the wooden door to the private office, glancing back at the brunette as he went in. She was still giggling delightedly into the telephone. He closed the door and turned his attention to the man behind the desk. The chair was swivelled so that Plasky's back was toward the door. His feet were crossed atop a low window-ledge and he was half-lying in the chair, the telephone clasped loosely to his head. He was telling the receptionist an off-color story, and vastly enjoying the telling.

Bolan dropped into a leather chair and lit a cigarette. Plasky ended the story with an explosive laugh, then launched immediately into another, swivelling about and raising his voice to share it with his visitor. Despite the high-humored jocularity of the moment, Bolan was aware that he was being sized up, and he did some sizing himself. Plasky was a heavy man, but not soft, thick of chest and shoulders. The hand clasping the telephone was a powerful one with stubby, squared-off fingers—well manicured. Bolan aged the man at about forty. The hair was light brown, nearly blonde, and carefully barbered. A chiselled, ruddy face completed the not-unhandsome picture.

Bolan grinned with the punch line of the story and could hear the delighted shrieking of the brunette rattling the diaphragm of the telephone receiver. Plasky dropped the instrument, the genial lines of his face instantly reforming into a cool composure as his eyes locked onto his visitor's.

"The day's contribution to employee relations," he explained in a suddenly businesslike voice. "You're Bolan, eh?" he asked, with hardly a pause.

The visitor nodded. "*Mack* Bolan. I won't be in town long. Figured I better get this business settled."

Plasky fussed with a manila folder that lay unopened on his desk. "It was good of you to contact us," he said. "Course—you understand our circumstances. Uh—we're an *auditing* firm. You understand that. The unfortunate —uh—circumstances—over at Triangle Industrial . . ."

"I won't be in town long," Bolan repeated. "I was told that you are temporarily in charge of the Triangle accounts."

"Wasn't that a terrible thing?" Plasky muttered. "Five good men—imagine that—some nut, some lunatic, and five good men—wiped out—just like *that!*" He snapped thick fingers in emphasis. "I—uh—I've got your father's book here, Mr. Bolan," he went on, in subdued tones. He flipped up the front cover of the manila folder, stared briefly at something inside, then closed it again. "Frankly, this account is in a mess. Your father is in serious arrears."

Bolan produced a small spiral notebook and tossed it onto the desk. "Not according to this," he said. "That's my father's record. He borrowed four hundred dollars eleven months ago. He has repaid five hundred and fifty. And I have reason to believe that other payments, not recorded in his book, have been made by other members of the family. Obviously your books are in error."

Plasky smiled blandly and spread his hands, palms up, on the desktop, ignoring Bolan's notebook. "Loan companies are not charitable institutions, Mr. Bolan, and let me assure you—we do not make errors in our books. Each account is double-audited, and—"

"He borrowed four, he repaid five-and-a-half. The debt should be paid."

Plasky was working diligently at the smile. "Your confusion is understandable, soldier." He was reminding Bolan of his lower place in the order of intelligence. "Like I said, financiers are not charity-minded. They rent out their money. It's a simple rental arrangement. If you rent a house or a car, you expect to pay your rent each month and also to return the property—*all* of the property—when your rental period has expired. Right?"

Bolan merely nodded.

"We rented your father a sum of money. The rental period specified was ninety days. If your father had returned our property at the expiration of that period, and if his rent was all paid up at that time, the debt would have been settled. But he did not. Naturally, in any business arrangement, there are certain penalty agreements to be invoked when one of the parties defaults. So many people fail to understand the financial structure of the business world. Now all your father has managed to do is to barely keep up the *rent* payments and to pay some of the penalties. He *still* has *all* of the property he rented—in this case, *our* money. We want it back. Are we so unreasonable?"

"Five hundred and fifty bucks is pretty high rent on *four hundred* bucks, isn't it?" Bolan observed softly.

"You're forgetting the penalties," Plasky shot back. He smiled. "All right, you're an intelligent man, Mr. Bolan. Sure, our interest rates are high. We provide a service at a risk that few financiers would be interested in. Why didn't your father borrow this money from a bank? Huh? You know the answer to that. No bank would have risked a nickel on your father. We did. We risked four hundred dollars on him. Frankly, soldier, your old man was a bad risk. Naturally our interest rates have to take that cruel fact into account. And, of course, we don't *force* anyone to do business with us. We—"

"You keep saying 'we,'" Bolan interrupted. "I thought—"

"Plasky Enterprises is associated with Triangle, of course," Plasky said. "Shall we get down to business now? Are you prepared to settle your father's account?"

"As far as I'm concerned it's already settled," Bolan replied mildly. "I just came in to tell you that."

"Our business is with your father, Mr. Bolan," Plasky said, coloring furiously. "He'll have to talk for himself."

"That'd be a pretty good trick, Mr. Plasky. He was buried ten days ago."

There was a moment of silence as Plasky whipped the cover of the Bolan account open and closed several times. Finally he said, "We'll just refer the matter to our legal department. We can tie up the estate, you know."

"There's no estate and you know it," Bolan told him. "The debt is paid, Plasky. He got four, he returned five and a half. The debt is paid." He rose to leave.

"You don't know what you're saying, fella," Plasky sneered, rising with him.

"Is your *legal department* going to pack up their brass knucks and follow me to Vietnam?" Bolan asked, his tone faintly mocking.

"Vietnam?" the other man echoed.

"I got emergency leave to bury the old man. I'll be going back in a couple of days. By the way . . ." Bolan sat back down.

"Yeah?" The ruddy face was further flushed with suppressed anger.

"I saw those guys get it."

"What? What guys?"

"The guys down at Triangle. I saw them die."

"So?" Plasky's hands were clenched together on the desk.

"I think I saw the guy that did it."

An electric silence settled into the atmosphere of the sumptuous office. Plasky's knuckles cracked, emphasizing the silence. "Did you go to the police?" he asked presently.

"And get involved in a mess like that?" Bolan's tone clearly implied that such an action was unthinkable.

"My—uh—associates would be interested in your—uh —observations."

"Like I said, I'm going to Vietnam in a couple of days," Bolan replied.

"I—uh—could set up a quick meeting."

"I want some fun and frolic before I go back to the jungle rot," the tall man mused. "I don't want to get tied up."

"I guarantee you all the fun and frolic you can handle," Plasky replied quickly, reaching for the telephone.

Bolan's hand stopped him. "Then there's this other thing," he said.

"What other thing?"

"This strained customer relation thing. I say the Bolan debt is settled."

"Of course! Of course it's settled!"

"I want the note."

Plasky dug into the folder, produced an imposingly legal-appearing paper, and slid it into Bolan's hand. The tall man glanced at it, then settled back in his chair with a grunt, folding the paper and placing it in a pocket. Plasky's stubby forefinger stabbed into the telephone dial.

"Do you believe in fate, Bolan?" Plasky asked, obviously highly pleased with the turn of the morning's events.

"Yeah. You'd never believe how much I believe in fate, Mr. Plasky," the tall man replied.

And The Executioner smiled.

2—The Plan

Mack Bolan had no illusions regarding his self-appointed task. He was no starry-eyed crusader. Neither was he a vengeance-ridden zealot. "No monkeys on my back," was his realistic motto. He did not necessarily believe in dying for just causes; he simply felt that a man would do his duty as he saw it. Perhaps this was a family trait, and perhaps it was just as subject to erroneous application as the recent actions of his sister, his brother, and his father. But Mack Bolan's duty seemed rather clear-cut to him at the present.

He saw a cancerous leech at the throat of America, and he saw the inability or the indisposition of American institutions to deal with it. He saw, also, that he was both equipped and positioned to strike a telling blow to at least one small tentacle of the monster growth. To a man like Mack Bolan this was a clear call to duty. But there were no illusions. He was aware of the hazards, of the odds against his success. He was in violation of the law himself, of course. Already, in the eyes of his society, he was a five-time murderer.

If apprehended he could expect little sympathy from the courts of law. Already the police might be sniffing hotly along his trail. He had proved to himself, through the visit to Plasky's office, that *"the organization"* also was strongly interested in the Triangle Industrial killings. He was satisfied in his own mind that they had their contacts, both in and out of society, and a strong intelligence capability that would soon lead them inevitably to Mack Bolan.

But his visit to Plasky Enterprises was not an act of

foolish bravado nor of amateurish bumbling. He knew precisely what he was doing, or what he was attempting. He was moving against the enemy in a coolly careful battle plan. *Seek and destroy*. This was the plan. Find, identify, then execute—before they can regroup and counterattack. At the moment he had the advantage. He had to press that advantage. He had found the link beyond Triangle Industrial. The battle plan now called for an infiltration through that link.

Infiltration!

Target Identification!

Confirmation!

DESTRUCTION!

This was the plan. Somewhere in that tangle he would find a man called Leo. And Bolan had to admit that he was looking forward to that meeting with something more than a cool sense of duty. Leo, too, was part of the plan.

3—Point of Law

Lieutenant of Detectives Al Weatherbee glared unseeingly at the stack of departmental reports that occupied the exact center of his desk, chewed thoughtfully on his lower lip for a moment, then surged up out of the chair and directed his 200-odd pounds in the general direction of the closed door. He paused in midstride, returned to the desk, pawed through the reports, and extracted a single sheet, reread it, grunted, returned it to the stack, then continued the interrupted journey to the door. He opened it, caught the eye of a dark-skinned man who sat just outside, and said, "Bring in that soldier now, Jack." He left the door ajar and went back to his chair, behind the desk. He had lit a cigarette and was staring again at the imposing stack of papers at desk-center when a uniformed officer entered with another uniformed man beside him. Weatherbee glanced at the tall figure and grimaced, a twisting of the lips and cheeks that could be construed as a smile.

"You want me to stay, Lieutenant?" the policeman asked.

Weatherbee shook his head in a terse negative and rose with hand outstretched toward the tall man in the U.S. Army uniform. "I'm Lieutenant Weatherbee," he said. "Sit down, Sergeant Bolan."

The tall man shook hands, then dropped into a plain wooden chair that was placed against the side of the desk, and leaned forward tensely with hands clasped atop his legs, peering intently into the detective's eyes. Weatherbee waited for the door to close, then he smiled engagingly and said, "That's an interesting collection of fruit salad." He leaned forward to study the military decoration on the soldier's breast. "I recognize the Purple Heart and the marksman's medal—and, yeah, the Bronze Star—the rest of 'em are out of my era, I guess. How many weapons have you qualified as expert on?"

Bolan met the suddenly penetrating gaze. "Just about all the personal weapons," he replied.

"Are you expert enough to get off five shots in less than five seconds, with a perfect score at better than a hundred yards?"

"Depends on the weapon," Bolan said easily. "I've done it."

"With a lever-action piece?"

"We don't use lever-actions in the Army," Bolan replied soberly.

"Uh-huh." Weatherbee took a drag from his cigarette and exhaled noisily. "I've had a couple of Telex conversations with a friend of mine in Saigon. You know a Major Harrington?"

Bolan shook his head negative.

"Military Police in Saigon. Knew each other back when. Told me something interesting about you, Sergeant." The detective's face hardened somewhat. He dropped the cigarette into an ashtray and raised probing eyes to the soldier's face. "Said they have a nickname for you back there, in your old outfit. Said they call you 'The Executioner.' Why would they call you something like that, Sergeant?"

Bolan shifted his weight in the chair and let his eyes wander about the police officer's face for a brief moment. Then, "If you're playing games with me, sir, shouldn't I at least be told the name of the game?"

"The name of the game is *homicide*," Weatherbee snapped.

"Every man I killed in Vietnam was in the line of duty," Bolan replied lightly.

"This isn't Vietnam!" Weatherbee said. "And a sniper cannot walk the streets of this city deciding who should live and who should not!"

Bolan shrugged. "If you're trying to connect me with that shooting the other night—just because I'm an expert marksman . . ."

"Not *just* because!" the policeman retorted. "Now look, Bolan—you were in here the other day raising hell with Captain Howard over this Triangle outfit, claiming they were responsible for your old man going berserk! You—"

"Aren't you the one who headed up that investigation?" Bolan broke in. "I mean, the deaths of my family?"

Weatherbee opened his mouth, then closed it and gave his head a curt affirmative nod.

"Then you saw," the soldier said simply. "And you know why it happened. And nobody made a move against the leeches. Until last night. Somebody finally made a move. So who's to complain? The papers call it a gangland tiff. Who cares who did it, so long as it got done?"

Weatherbee glared at him through a long silence. Then he crushed out his cigarette, lit another, sighed, and said softly, "*I* care, Bolan. Justice isn't perfect in this country, but by God it's the best justice under the law that can be found anywhere. We can't have self-appointed judges and juries walking the streets with guns in their hands. Hell, man, this isn't Vietnam!"

"If I am being accused of a crime, isn't there a formality to be observed?" Bolan said, his features rigid in a set smile.

"You aren't being charged," the lieutenant replied. "Not yet. But I know exactly what happened, Bolan. You understand that. I know. I know that some one broke into The Hunt Shop on August 18th, took a shiny new .444 calibre Marlin lever-action rifle and a powerful scope. I know that he took the rifle out to the old quarry to sight it in. We know that *somebody* was out there for two hours on the morning of August 19th, firing methodically in bursts of five along three precise ranges—one of a hundred yards, another a hundred and ten, and one a hundred and twenty yards. The caretaker didn't think much about it until he saw the papers yesterday morning, and I won't insult your intelligence by trying to make you think he got close enough to identify anybody. Just so you'll know I'm not playing games with you, Sarge.

"Then two days ago our marksman went up to the fourth floor of the Delsey Building. He sat in an open window of an empty office. He smoked four Pall Malls—*your* brand, I see—and he used a Coke bottle for an ash tray. At almost exactly six o'clock he levered five soft-nosed slugs into the street below, with the punch of a bear-gun, and the Triangle Industrial Finance Company suddenly went temporarily out of business. . . . And vengeance is mine, saith The Executioner."

The lanky sergeant shifted his weight, causing the chair to creak beneath him. "If you *know* so much," he said softly, "why aren't you charging me?"

"Would you like to make a statement?"

"Not unless I'm under arrest."

"You know you're not under arrest."

"Then I have no statement," Bolan said, smiling tightly.

"What sort of screwy ideas you got in that noodle of yours, Sarge?"

Bolan held his hands up, palms out. "No screws whatsoever," he replied.

"When are you due back in Vietnam?"

"I'm not due back." Bolan grinned engagingly. "New orders came yesterday. Humanitarian reassignment."

"Reassignment *where?*" Weatherbee asked quickly.

"To the ROTC Unit at Franklin High, right here in Pittsfield."

"Aw *shit!*" the policeman exploded.

"Because of the kid brother," Bolan added meekly. "I'm his only kin."

Weatherbee charged to his feet and paced the floor between the desk and the door, working furiously at a sudden charge of static energy. "Well, this just complicates the hell out of things," he said presently. "I thought you'd be tucked securely away in those jungles and out of my hair." He stabbed a finger to punctuate each word as he added, "The front lines of Vietnam would be the most humanitarian assignment you could get!"

"I don't know what you're talking about," Bolan said uneasily.

"Sure you do, you know what I'm talking about. I'm talking about the Mafia, an organization that cant afford to forgive and forget. I'm talking about a guy known as 'The Executioner,' who may or may not have executed five of their number—and those guys don't give anybody the benefit of any doubts the way the law does. I'm talking about the streets of my city becoming a shooting gallery, and of my inability to do anything but sit on the sidelines and watch like a spectator because I don't have any physical evidence to take into a court of law.

"I'm levelling with you, Sarge. Understand this! You're up the creek whether you're guilty or not! You *look* guilty as sin—maybe not guilty enough for a court of law, but guilty sure as hell enough for the law of the Mafia! They may not get to you today, or even tomorrow, but believe me they *will* get to you. And I'm sidelined. Understand? I can't do a thing to help you—even saying I wanted to. So what becomes of the kid brother now, eh? What becomes of the kid brother with your blood filling my gutters, Bolan?"

"What would be your suggestion?" Bolan asked, eyeing the other sharply.

"Give me a statement. A confession. It's the only way you can get the protection of the law."

Bolan laughed tartly. "Some protection. All the way to the electric chair, eh? And *then* what becomes of the kid brother, eh, Weatherbee?"

"I don't think it'd be that rough. There *are* circumstances."

"Sure. *Sure*, there are." Bolan got to his feet. "You're playing games with me, Lieutenant. If I'm free to go . . ."

"Look, soldier, I don't have a case on you," the policeman fumed. "Am I being honest? How much more honest can a cop get? I can't take a war hero into court on nothing more than a hunch and a couple of suspicions. I don't have enough evidence to get an indictment. But I can't forget that a guy like you is prowling my streets, 'The Executioner' for Christ's sake, with a hard-on for the mob. And don't think for one small second that *they* can forget it, either."

"Well—thanks for the honesty," Bolan said. He smiled. "See you around." He opened the door and walked out, nodded his head at the uniformed officer, and made for the open doorway at the other end of the large room. Pausing as he rounded the corner, he tossed a glance over his shoulder. The big plainclothesman was leaning against his doorjamb, hands thrust deeply into pockets, gazing disconsolately after him. A sudden chill shot down Bolan's spine, and he knew a moment of self-doubt.

Was he overestimating his own capabilities? Could he really expect to wage any sort of an effective one-man war on an organization that even the collective talents and technologies of the world's police were helpless against? Bolan shrugged and went on down the stairs. There was no turning back. The war was already on. And The Executioner had an afternoon appointment with some of the inner circle. The law had made its point. But The Executioner wasn't buying it.

4—An Equal Opportunity

It could have been any gathering of successful businessmen, relaxing in a country club atmosphere. The florid face of Nat Plasky was just a shade lighter than the crimson slash of swim trunks that separated his hairy mass into seemingly equal parts. He leaned against a poolside cabana, a sweating glass of iced liquid held carelessly and seemingly forgotten in a massive paw, engaged in quiet conversation with an eye-jerking blonde young woman in an almost nonexistent bikini. Several other dazzling Miss Universe types, displaying various ideas of the nude swimwear look behind fishnet, nudie panels, and enchantingly strategic placements of mini-materials, sprawled here and there beside the pool. Nobody appeared to be wet, nor inclined to get that way.

A suave man of about fifty, carefully attired in white duck trousers, canvas sneakers, and a polo shirt sat at an umbrella table with a younger man who wore slacks, a turtle-neck shirt, and a light sports jacket. Several other men wandered about aimlessly, almost blending into the background of sunning platforms, plastic flotation devices, and colorful cabanas—*bodyguards*, was Bolan's quick impression. And they were watching him. Some unspoken signal or herd instinct prompted all eyes present to swing toward Bolan as he approached the pool. Plasky waved his glass in Bolan's direction, said something to the blonde, and hurried forward to greet the new arrival.

"We been invaded by the U.S. Army," one girl murmured lazily, eyeing the tall soldier with interest.

"Shut up, stupid," Plasky grunted as he brushed past her. He went to Bolan with hand outstretched, then led the soldier like a long-lost friend to the table where the two other men sat. "Walt Seymour, this is Sergeant Mack Bolan," he intoned formally, presenting Bolan to the older man first. The obvious protocol was not lost on Bolan. He smiled and extended his hand, aware that he had progressed at least one step above Plasky, and also aware that he was receiving a firm but uninvolved grip of social courtesy only. The younger man seized Bolan's hand as soon as it was free and wrung it enthusiastically. It was the sort of handshake Bolan could understand, and he swept the man with a warm gaze.

"I'm Leo Turrin," the warm one said, smiling. "Hear you're just back from 'Nam. Welcome home. What outfit you with over there?"

"Ninth Infantry," Bolan replied, hoping he hadn't reacted to the other's name. He'd recognized the comradely tone of another returned veteran, and the face meant nothing in his memory, but Johnny Bolan's words, *this guy she called Leo*, were dizzying his inner ear.

"I was in the Green Berets," Turrin was saying chattily. "I was a sergeant, too. Specialist-fifth, anyway."

Bolan recognized also the value of the common-interest tie with this obviously "in" member of the circle. He grinned and tried a long shot. "I always heard the most valuable specialists in the Berets were the female-procurers," he said.

The remark scored right on target. Turrin did a double-take toward the suavely poised Seymour, then exploded in a fit of laughter, digging an elbow toward Bolan. "Well, I'll tell you—" he cried, then abruptly quietened upon receipt of a coldly disapproving glare from Seymour. The ex-GI winked at Bolan and dropped back into his chair.

One of the near-nudies appeared at that moment and thrust a frosted glass into Bolan's hand. He thanked her and sat down at Plasky's invitation, directly across from Seymour. "Beautiful girl," Bolan murmured appreciatively.

"Aren't they all," Plasky said boredly. "You like her, she's yours. *After* we've finished our business." He glanced at the swaying tail section of the girl as she retreated toward the cabanas, as though wondering if he'd missed something.

Bolan noticed that the bodyguards had settled down, apparently on some prearranged station. "Then let's get on with the business," he said, grinning.

Plasky cleared his throat and dropped his eyes toward his own drink. "Seymour and Turrin and I were business associates of Joseph Laurenti. One of the men who were murdered. And of course we knew all five—almost like family, you might say. We are very much interested in—helping the police bring the killer to justice. Have you talked to the police yet, Sergeant Bolan?"

Bolan was expecting the question, especially in view of the fact that he had been picked up that morning almost in the shadow of Plasky's office, and he was prepared for it. "Yes, they pulled me in this morning," he replied. "Right after I left your office."

"You went to them voluntarily," Seymour declared quietly.

Bolan grinned. "Not hardly."

"Why not?" Seymour wanted to know.

"Like I told Mr. Plasky, I didn't want to get tied up in something that would spoil my last few days at home." He broadened the smile. "As it turns out, I'm not going back to 'Nam after all. I've been reassigned. I'll be staying right here in Pittsfield for a while."

"Why?" Seymour persisted.

"My kid brother. He's only fourteen. I'm his sole surviving relative."

"That was very good of the Army," Plasky put in.

Seymour ignored the goodness of the Army. "So you decided to cooperate fully with the police," he commented. "After you left Mr. Plasky this morning and received word of your good fortune, you immediately contacted the police like any upstanding citizen would wish to do."

Bolan was still grinning. "You don't listen very well, do you. I told you I was pulled in. When I left Plasky this morning, a squad car was pulled up behind my U-Drive. A homicide detective wanted to talk to me."

"Why?" Seymour was beginning to sound hung-up on the word.

"One of those odd coincidences," Bolan replied, sobering. "The same cop who investigated my father's death is working this Triangle thing. He—"

"Your father was murdered also?" Seymour asked quickly.

"Suicide," Bolan said. "Nervous breakdown or something, I don't know. He was despondent and he was sick and he was deeply in debt. This homicide cop remembered that one of the debts was with Triangle. He was just wondering if there could be a connection, if maybe *I* might be the guy with the quick gun. He called me in to talk about it." Bolan realized he was skating close to a precipice, and hoped he wasn't overdoing the open-face routine. He smiled. "Hell, I don't settle money debts with a gun." He nodded toward Plasky. "You can vouch for that. Anyway, I satisfied the cop's curiosity. He thanked me for coming in, and that was that."

"You're leaving something out," Seymour said lazily.

"Yeah?"

"Yeah. Sam Bolan gunned down his wife and daughter, too."

"Hey, take it easy, Walt," Turrin said softly.

"It's all right," Bolan snapped, his eyes steady on Seymour. "I don't hold it against my pop for doing what he did. Look—I cut out as soon as I was old enough. The less said about the women in my family the better. Okay?"

Seymour and Turrin exchanged glances. *They know*, Bolan decided.

"Sure, I understand, Sarge," Seymour replied quickly. "Don't mind me, I'm just trying to get your size. Okay?"

"Okay. You got it?"

"I think so. Why don't you tell us your eyewitness version of this killing now, eh?"

Bolan glared at him. "Why should I do *you* any favors, eh?"

"Well—after all ..." Perplexed, Seymour massaged his nose, then chuckled. "You're the one brought the whole thing up," he said. "And you did come all the way out here to my home to talk about it. Didn't you?"

"No."

"No?" Seymour's eyebrows rose and his eyes angled toward Plasky.

Bolan calmly lit a cigarette, blew the smoke straight up, and said, "The cops changed all that."

"I see," Seymour said. But it was obvious that he did not see.

"I did see something. I was down there when the shooting occurred. I saw this guy come running out of the Delsey Building. We nearly collided."

"So?" Plasky asked ominously.

"So I could never go on record with a story like that. It places me at the scene, and with Weatherbee wondering about me I can't afford to be placed at the scene."

"Who is Weatherbee?" Seymour wanted to know.

"A homicide detective."

Seymour sighed and grinned at Plasky. "We don't want you to go on record, Sergeant. We wouldn't place your information in the hands of the police."

"I know that."

"You do?"

Bolan nodded. "But it doesn't change anything. Look, my original idea was to sell you people the information. That's all changed now. The cops told me who you are, see. And that changed everything."

Seymour flashed a glance toward Plasky. "And just who are we?"

"You're the Mafia."

Seymour's smile faded. Plasky coughed. Turrin's fingers began drumming against the table. "We're the *what?*" Seymour muttered.

"Hell, it's common knowledge," Bolan said. "With the cops, I guess. They told me that Triangle is tied in with the Mafia."

"So what kind of game are you playing, soldier boy?" Plasky hissed.

"Down, Nat, down," Seymour hurried in. He turned appraising eyes onto Bolan. "Just suppose the cops were right about that connection. How would that change anything?"

"It changes my price," Bolan said, soberly returning Seymour's gaze.

Turrin chuckled and relaxed into his chair. Plasky snorted and said something unintelligible. Seymour reacted not at all. Finally he sighed and said, "Either you're mighty smart or mighty damn dumb, Bolan. Just what *is* the game?"

"The game," Bolan replied slowly, "is that I can identify your killer for you. And suddenly I realize that's the *last* thing you want. You don't *want* any identification. Look—I have no argument with you. I know how these things go. I don't know anything about the beef between you and Laurenti, but I do understand discipline. If Laurenti was trying to pull a fast one, then you only did what had to be done. I just want *you* to understand that I'm no blabbermouth. Not around cops. So—the price is changed. There is no price. There is no eyewitness story. I *saw* nothing and I *say* nothing."

Plasky's jaw had dropped. He turned surprised eyes onto Seymour and grunted, "This guy thinks—"

"I know what he thinks!" Seymour snapped. "It's been obvious all along." His gaze had not strayed from the faintly amused face of the soldier. "There was no beef," he informed Bolan. "Regardless of what the newspapers said, Laurenti and his people were not killed by any criminal organization. So you're wasting your time and ours with your little game. If you'll just—"

"How about playing the game with the cards face up," Bolan suggested.

"What are your cards, Sergeant?" Seymour asked, eyes twinkling at Plasky.

"I'm job hunting. Five of your people stopped living yesterday. I figure you have a vacancy."

Turrin shifted uneasily. "What does a soldier need with a job?" Plasky asked faintly.

"I've been twelve years in this uniform," Bolan replied. "I've learned a trade, but it hasn't made me any money. I don't have a dime, and I'll never have a dime, not from what this uniform will bring me."

Seymour was beginning to warm up. "What sort of a trade?" he inquired.

"Guns are my business."

"Guns?" Seymour laughed softly. "You think guns are our business?"

Bolan ignored the parry. "I can build them, I can modify them, I can repair them, I can make the ammo for them, and I can shoot them."

Seymour was still clucking. "Even supposing that we *are* what you *think* we are, you have your eras confused. This isn't Chicago of the twenties and thirties. This is Pittsfield of the sixties." He shook his head. "You've got us all wrong, Sergeant."

Bolan nodded his head toward a background man who was positioned in the shadow of a poolside cabana. "*He's* wearing a gun," he said, then stabbed his finger toward the diving platform, and added, "so's that one. I counted five gun-bearers the instant I stepped onto this property. You've got a civilian army here. And you've got vacancies. And I need a job."

"You planning on deserting from the Army?" Turrin put in.

The soldier soberly shook his head. "You know what an ROTC billet is, Turrin? It's a cream-pie duty."

"Tell us about it," Seymour said interestedly.

"That's my humanitarian reassignment. To the ROTC unit out here at Franklin High. The Army supplies instructors for these programs. It's cream-pie duty for any soldier. We get a housing allowance, we work regular hours, just like any teacher, and we live like any civilian."

"These regular hours—how do you figure to work two jobs at once?"

Bolan grinned. "I'm not the regular instructor. I'm just padded on to give me an official duty station. There's already a guy out there. I'll just be an odd hand. Maybe I'll give a few lectures on gun handling, maybe I'll help out a little on the rifle range. But I was given to understand that I'd be more or less free to come and go as I please."

"Don't sound like the Army to me," Turrin said, smiling.

"Me either," Bolan agreed. "But I'll be up for re-enlistment at the end of the year. And there's this responsibility for the kid brother, see. They're giving me until the end of the year to make some provisions for him. I guess they figure by then I'll either have to return to full duty or just get the hell out of the Army."

"I should think you'd be quite happy with the arrangement," Seymour observed.

"Well, I've got the kid now," Bolan pointed out. "And like I said, not a dime in any bank. I figure I'll take the discharge in December. And I can't see any sense in wasting any time getting phased into civilian life." He smiled broadly. "And then, you've got this vacancy."

"I think the sarge is a conniving opportunist," Seymour said, to nobody in particular.

"We need opportunists—that's what we need, isn't it?" Turrin said.

Seymour sighed. "Yeah, yeah, that's exactly what we need. Well—get those girls over here, Leo. And roll that bar over here. It seems we have a new employee to welcome." He smiled sourly at Bolan. "This is your day of golden opportunity, Sarge. Don't let it turn to brass."

Bolan grinned and picked up his drink. It had become tepid and flat. Who cared? Hell, who cared? He gulped it down. He was in. And from the looks of things he was about to get into something else. Her name, somebody told him, was Mara; her function was entirely obvious. She settled into his lap without an invitation, handing him a fresh drink, and wriggled the bikini-clad—or almost-clad—bottom about in an apparent striving for comfort, at the expense of Bolan's own. "I like soldiers," she confided softly, running a hand inside his shirt. The bikini barely topped the swell of her lower abdomen, a thin stretch of elastic traversing the centerline of belled hips and plunging in back well below the pronounced cleft of swollen buttocks. The halter of the bikini was no more than an elasticized scrap of overlaid "now you see it, now you don't" netting. Bolan's free hand found a natural resting place on the silky torso at a point about midway between the upper and lower edges of the "swim" suit, fingers splayed down across the soft indentation of the navel. He flicked a glance around in a brief survey of his companions, noted that they were comparably burdened and preoccupied, then let his fingers travel on southward.

The girl giggled and captured his hand, raised slightly off his lap to gaze beneath her, and murmured: "You haven't been around women lately, have you?" She then resettled, again agitating herself into the closest possible conjunction and moving Bolan's hand up and onto her breast. "Have you forgotten what those feel like?" she asked whimsically.

Bolan nudged the net aside and assured her that he had, indeed, not forgotten. She giggled, took the drink out of his hand, set it on the nearby table and slid off his lap, then playfully tugged him out of the chair. "We need to get you into a pair of trunks," she told him. She moved close alongside and beneath his arm, maintaining a tight, lock-step embrace, and steered him to a cabana. She entered with him, locked the door, and moved immediately into his arms, raising her mouth to his. He took it hungrily, suddenly aware of how long it had been since a vibrant American girl had been in his arms. Her breath was sweetly alcoholic, hot and wanting, altogether pleasant, an active tongue probing for effect. Spring-tension hips were thrust high and forward and moving rhythmically for an even more disturbing effect. His hands fell onto bunched buttocks, then he hooked his thumbs into the hips and flipped her away, breaking also the hot conjuncture of mouths.

She swayed back in for more. He evaded her, the thinking part of his brain seemingly numbed and reacting instinctively. "Afraid you'll mess up your pants?" she murmured. One of her hands moved between them, and she said, "Uh-huh. You've been too long without, Sarge." She moved away from him then, swinging her attention to the far wall of the small hut. An assortment of male swimming trunks hung from pegs there. Her eyes returned to his midsection, sizing him, then she selected from the swimwear. "Put these on," she suggested, tossing the trunks onto a low bench behind Bolan.

Bolan was still feeling somewhat mechanical in his actions. His fingers were already at his shirtfront, working the buttons. She moved back to him and went to work on the tie. A moment later she carefully hung shirt and tie on a peg, pushed him onto the bench, and took off his shoes and socks.

"I don't give this service to just everybody," she told

him, smiling darkly. Her hands seized his belt. "You're different."

He pushed her hands away and got to his feet. "Everybody's different," he grunted, his thinking faculties returning. He was fumbling with the waistband of his trousers. "I'll be out in a minute," he added, giving her a meaningful gaze.

"You don't really mean that," the girl replied. A quick motion of her hands caused the bikini bra to fall away. Glistening cones sprang forward, jiggling tauntingly in the sudden release, the pale pink at the tips highlighting the projection. She cupped them in her hands, gently agitating the nipples with her thumbs, which were already protruding slightly; they grew noticeably under the attention, riveting Bolan's eyes in fascinating inspection. "That net makes them itch," she explained. "Wouldn't you like to scratch them for me?"

Without a word, Bolan reached forward and tugged down the bikini panties. She stepped out of them with a throaty giggle and reached for his trousers, expertly lowering shorts and all in one brief motion and falling against him, moving sensually for calculated effect. Bolan groaned and clasped her to him, luxuriating in the fusion of male and female flesh. Her arms went tightly about him, hands rubbing feverishly at his back, piledriving hips once again in action. Bolan twisted out of the embrace, his breathing harsh and ragged.

"It *has* been a while," he admitted.

"Don't worry about that," she said, obviously enjoying the explosiveness of the encounter. There was no room to stretch out in the tiny dressing room; it was also obvious that she had dealt with similar situations before. She pulled the little bench around and pushed Bolan down onto it, seated on the end, then she climbed aboard, straddling man and bench, seizing and stuffing him in with an obviously practiced maneuver and settling onto him with a harsh bounce. Bolan experienced an immediate tremor, his arms going about her and squeezing her fiercely to him as his back sought the surface of the bench. She went down with him, murmuring, "Good, good."

It had happened so quickly as to seem totally unreal to Bolan. "I don't suppose that did much for you, eh," he muttered apologetically.

She lay there, the magnificent breasts spreading across his chest, lips nibbling at his neck, entirely relaxed.

"It can wait," she told him. "You guys always come back full of TNT or something." She struggled to her feet, smiling ruefully at his midsection, pulled a towel from a shelf and dropped it onto him.

"Are you a prostitute?" he asked her, point-blank.

She blinked at him, then smiled. "Sure," she said, still smiling.

"Then it really doesn't matter to you, does it. I mean . . ."

"I know what you mean." She retrieved the male trunks from the floor and tossed them at him, then began pulling on her own trunks. Then she stared at him silently for a long moment, picked up the bra, seemed to be debating something in her mind, then hung the bra on a wall peg. "But you're wrong," she said suddenly. "It does matter. And I'll show you. It will be better next time. Now that you're de-charged. Well—come on. Let's take a swim. And after that . . . Well, we'll find a better place than this damn shack. Okay?"

He grinned at her. "Okay," he said. He got into the trunks, and they both went out and took a topless dive into the pool. Bolan was looking forward to the next time, and the next place. Obviously, Mara was also. It was the most exhilarating swim Mack Bolan had ever taken.

5—A Master's Stroke

Walter Seymour was disturbed. It had not been easy to build a place for himself in the organization. Not with a name like Walter Seymour, for Christ's sake. Now if his name had been Giovanni Scalavini—or some such—the road would have been a lot smoother. Even Nat Plasky had an edge on him, purely because the name *sounded* better to the old guard—even though any idiot would know that Plasky was no wop. Seymour had outrun Laurenti quite simply because, right blood or not, Laurenti had never been and would never be anything more than a nickel-and-dime hood. He'd had a hood's intellect and a hood's heart—a perfect combination and an ideal mentality for the nickel-and-dime business of payday-loan collection. Seymour had never liked the Triangle operation. He was honest enough with himself to admit that what he'd disliked about it the most was Laurenti. The Triangle front provided a good repository for illegal dollars, and Seymour would have been content to see it run as a strictly legitimate loan company—it had been the mentality of Laurenti that made Triangle a brass-knucks operation. Laurenti simply had a loan-shark mentality—and, of course, Triangle was Laurenti's baby. He was a wop, and the old wops liked him, and his ties with the organization had extended back through several generations and even into the old country.

So—in a way—Seymour had been almost happy to see Laurenti dead. Not just from a personal viewpoint, he kept telling himself, but from the business angle as well. Laurenti, and Laurenti types, were bad for the organization. Seymour was glad he was dead. At the same time, Seymour was disturbed about those deaths. Who the hell had decided to gun down Laurenti and his people? Who the hell and *why* the hell?

Seymour was a realist. He knew that the "man upstairs" at Pittsfield had never fully accepted him. He'd been on probation for ten damn years, and nobody knew it better than Walt Seymour himself. Now if this damn GI, this Bolan guy, could come up with ideas of an organization rub-out, and if the press could think that way, and if the cops could think the same way—then for damn sure the man upstairs and all the men upstairs around the country might be thinking that way, too. It was no closely guarded secret that there had been bad blood between Seymour and Laurenti.

Yes, Walter Seymour was disturbed. He was disturbed about several things. The damn GI disturbed him. Even though he'd been thoroughly checked out and stamped genuine, there was something about the guy that just didn't ring. Walt Seymour was not "buying" Mack Bolan —not lock, stock, and barrel. Not for the moment, at least. Too many people, too damn many nosey people, were interested in the organization. Congressional committees, the Justice Department, the Treasury Department, the FBI—everybody had a big nose and an itching finger for the organization. And Walt Seymour was wondering about Mack Bolan's nose and fingers. Every manner of infiltration had been tried on them. The local cops had tried, the feds had tried, even other organizations had tried—but nobody had ever succeeded, not in any way that mattered. Walt Seymour was disturbed about Mack Bolan.

Something—*some*thing—just did not ring for Sergeant Mack Bolan. The best way to spot a phoney, in Seymour's mind, was to make a close inspection. The best way to inspect Mack Bolan was to get him on the payroll. Give him a loose leash, keep eyes, ears, and instincts open, and let the phoney reveal himself. Anybody could have sent him. Even the man upstairs could have sent him. Of course, if he was *not* a phoney—well, a guy like Bolan could be an asset to the organization. He could be an asset even to Seymour. Leo Turrin was beginning to give Seymour trouble. Turrin was smart, likeable, ambitious—and he had the right sound to his name. Yes, Walt Seymour was disturbed about Leo Turrin. He'd put Bolan with Turrin. It would be a masterful stroke, he decided. If Bolan *was* a phoney, then the man most likely to get hurt by him would be the man next to him. Yes. Yes. He'd put Bolan with Turrin. It would be a masterful stroke.

6—A Matter of Viewpoint

"The first thing you gotta remember," Turrin told Bolan, "is that I'm the C.O. You can think of yourself as the First Sergeant if you want to—but just remember that I'm the C.O. Then the second thing you gotta remember is that we *never* use the word 'Mafia'! Understand? It's 'The Organization.' You work for the organization and the organization works for you. That's the way it works. But you're not a member. You could never be a *member*. Your blood ain't right, see. Even Seymour ain't no *member*."

"There's a difference?" Bolan wanted to know.

They were in Turrin's automobile, a fancy canary-yellow convertible, and Turrin was giving his new protégé a lift home from Seymour's suburban home. "Sure there's a difference." He punched in the cigarette lighter and fished in his pocket for something to light, finally accepting a Pall Mall from Bolan. "Look, the organization goes back for centuries. Got started in Sicily, the home of my ancestors. It was sort of like Robin Hood, only this ain't no fairy tale, it's for real. I'll bet you didn't know—the Mafia is a real pure idea—real democracy, you know, democracy for the *little* people. For the ones that was getting *shit* on. It was even better than Robin Hood because it was a *mass* movement."

"No, I didn't know that," Bolan admitted.

"I'll bet you didn't know that 'Mafia' translates back to mean 'Matthew.' Matthew means 'brave, bold.' It had to be a secret society because it was going up against the establishment, see, the establishment of those olden times. There was tyranny, see, and all the money was divided up between the rich bastards, the noblemen, the aristocracy. All the laws were rigged to keep the poor people poor and the rich people rich. See? That's how all laws got started. Everywhere, not just in Italy and Sicily. Laws were written to protect the rich bastards, see. So these bold, brave guys got together in a resistance movement. They set up the Mafia, and it's been nip and tuck ever since."

"Hippies," Bolan grunted.

"What?"

"Early Italian hippies," Bolan said, grinning. "What were they demonstrating for—a pizza in every pot?"

Turrin's face clouded. "I don't think I like your sense of humor. I'm being serious. The Mafia is a very democratic idea."

"Okay, I'll be serious," Bolan replied. "But—uh—what's the moral of the thing, Leo? I mean, maybe a hundred years ago, in Italy or Sicily or wherever it was—okay, I can see the picture. But not over here. Not now. I mean, there *is* a democracy in this country. A *legal* democracy."

Turrin laughed lustily. "Shit!" he guffawed. "Don't let yourself get brainwashed. Things haven't changed that much. The rich still get richer while the poor get poorer. There's still a place here for the bold and the brave."

"Don't get me wrong," Bolan said. "I'm not arguing against the organization—hell, I'm part of it now. I just like to see things like they really are."

"Then see them like they really are. Don't get to feeling like a lousy criminal. You're the guy said you didn't have a dime to your name. Over there getting your ass shot off to protect the rich bastard's riches. See it like it is, Sarge. Didn't Seymour say he was starting you at two-fifty a week? Hell—does that sound like the poor getting poorer?"

The sergeant grinned. "Just call me Bolan the Bold, Captain."

Turrin turned him a warm gaze. "By Jesus, you'n me are gonna get along all right, Sarge—yes sir, *all* right."

"What *is* your operation, Leo?" Bolan wanted to know.

"Girls." He grinned delightedly.

Bolan felt suddenly light-headed. "Girls?" he echoed.

"Girls. All kinds'f girls. Hostess girls, party girls, call girls, house girls, street girls. Name your price range and I got just the girl for you."

"And they're all bold and brave too, eh?" Bolan asked, his tongue feeling strange and thick in his mouth.

"Betcher ass they are. You work for the organization, the organization works for you. We're spreading the riches around, see."

Bolan relaxed into the soft upholstery and closed his eyes. "Well, I guess that's one way of looking at it," he said quietly. He was thinking of another Bolan, and wondering just how brave she'd been, in there among the bold.

7—The Girl Watchers

Bolan was being worked into the routine that Turrin called "girl-watching." He had been outfitted in expensive civilian clothes and provided with a snub-nosed .32 calibre pistol, a license to carry same, and a shoulder-holster with a snap-out feature to carry it in. The clothing and the hardware had come from Bolan's future earnings; the gun license had appeared through some magical means wholly unknown to Bolan.

"It's legal, it's legal," Turrin assured him. "It ain't broadcasted, but it's legal, and if the question is ever raised about you carrying a gun, they'll find your license all duly recorded and all that jazz. So don't worry about it. We take care of those little details. Nobody gets nothing on the organization."

Turrin was operating behind a front called "Escorts Unlimited." The offices were swank and convincing and the "social" rooms of the "clubhouse" beyond reproach. He had a genuine computer match-making service, complete with certified programmer and staff.

"We make a little off the front," he confided to Bolan, "but just about enough to break even on the rent and salaries. We even carry a mortgage on that razzle-dazzle computer." He laughed. "Financed through Triangle Industrial Finance Company, that great little friend to free enterprisers."

Bolan discovered that his official job title was "security officer." He was on the legal payroll of Escorts Unlimited, and from his weekly $250 would routinely be deducted the social security and income taxes. "You can even have U.S. Savings Bonds taken out if you want," Turrin explained, "—but listen, don't worry about those legal deductions. We make all that up. You get an expense account, nontaxable, so don't worry. You come out all right. But we're legal, see. Strictly legal."

The undercover operation even had an air of legality about it. The various facets of organized prostitution in the city and surrounding suburbs were programmed into the computer and coded to insure against inadvertent loss of security and deliberate snooping. The program code for the call-girl operation, for example, was listed under "Dates Available by Prior Arrangement Only"—and the program "key" for specific informational or assignment "sorts" and "print-outs" was activated only by a secret code letter. The same file, sorted electronically and activated by the standard program code, would produce only a print-out on the legitimate dating service. Another operation was listed under "Dates by Spontaneous Selection," and a similar one as "Organized Social Activities"—covering, respectively, street girls and house girls.

"We use the machine, sure we use it," Turrin told Bolan. "Why not? The damn thing is foolproof, and you got no idea yet the *size* of this operation. I got hundreds of girls working the undercover end of things, and why should I try to keep all this stuff in my head, or in a secret set of books someplace. Listen, I got a 'destruct' I can punch into that computer and in *one second* there's not one incriminating record in the file—not one that anybody can get to, anyway. It wipes out everything but the legit operation. Hell, why shouldn't I use it? That's progress, Sarge—hell, that's sheer progress. My programmer calls it APPS, for Automated Prostitution Program System, and he's proud as hell of the thing. Hell, he's a scientist, that guy, a real *scientist*. The sweet part is that none of these people in the office, nobody but me and my programmer, know anything about the *real* business. The damn machine has even got *them* outsmarted. Not one of 'em could really testify to anything. It all looks on the up and up to *them*. So a guy calls in, see, and says he's John Smith of Ace Industries, and he's hosting a sales meeting. He wants us to send him a dozen hostesses to give the place some glitter. One of the office girls takes the order. If this guy is on the level then that's all there is to it. The girl runs the order through the program and she gets a list of names and phone numbers. She goes down the list, making the calls, until she fills the order. And everybody's happy. The sales meeting gets some pretty models to pretty things up and Escorts Unlimited has a happy customer. But—*but*—if this John Smith is *in the know* and he wants some bedsprings tigers for his little get-together, then he's got a *code* in his order that automatically triggers the computer to a *different* list. And he don't even know what the code is, it's just something my field man has rigged into his account number. Get the picture? The damn thing is foolproof. We change the program codes every day—*every damn day*—so we run things right up tight and we know who we're dealing with all the time.

"Another case. Say a guy is in town just for the night, and he wants some company. He lets it be known, just like a guy would in any town. You know, a word to the desk clerk or a waiter or a bellhop. You know the routine. In a matter of minutes one of my field men is on the horn, talking to one of the office girls. He places an order for a model, and he knows the program code to use. Sometimes in less than ten minutes a girl is on the job, and we got a happy client, and a totally dumb staff clerk who would testify on a stack of Bibles that all she ever did was call a free-lance model who's listed in our computer service. See? It's clean, it's clean as hell.

"We're pretty well protected from the girl end, too. There isn't much to tie her back to us, if she ever gets careless or unlucky. It's happened a couple of times, and we get very indignant, see. Imagine that! A *prostitute*, perverting our sacred service to ply her shameful trade!

Get the picture? We been took by the girl, see, and naturally we can't be responsible for anything like that."

"That doesn't say much for protection for the girl, does it?" Bolan inquired.

"Aw hell, they just get their wrists slapped. If it looks like she's in real trouble, you know, like they're gonna throw the book at her—why, we get her a lawyer—under the table, you know. We pay legal fees, or some of 'em, and we'll advance the money to cover fines. We take care of our girls. Unless they're *way* outta line. You work for the organization, the organization works for you. Remember that, Bolan the Bold. When the girls are okay to come back to work again, we run 'em into the computer with a new name and a new district and that's that. But you can see the security of the thing, can't you? I mean, we're *covered*, Sarge."

Beside Turrin and the programmer there were five other organization men in the operation, these five respectfully classified as "sales representatives" and referred to as "field men." The job title sounded better than "pimp" but the effect was precisely the same, even though much of their contact work was in the rarefied strata of big business, conventioneering, and politics.

"These are sharp boys," Turrin reported proudly. "—most of them are better educated than me. They can move around in the best circles, and in fact they *got* to. They hardly ever see their girls, and probably not one girl in ten would know any of these guys if they saw 'em at the same party, or even in the same bed. The field men work on a commission, so they're go-getters. They don't have a lot of contact with the street girls or the house girls, and damn little to do with their own party girls and call girls. We're *up tight* all the way, Sarge."

"With everything run so impersonally," Bolan probed, "I suppose you never have contact with any of these girls either, eh?"

Turrin winked and smiled knowingly. "Don't worry,

my sergeant, you'll have all the female flesh you can stomach." He laughed. "I make personal contact when I feel the need to. Not so much with the girls on the top end. Oh—" He frowned. "—sometimes a certain personal touch is called for. Sometimes I take a personal interest in a new girl, to get her started off right. You know." He laughed again. "But I got a wife and three kids, you know. I mean, I don't lay around with whores *all* the time."

Bolan dug his elbow into the other's ribs. "Hell, I bet you got a dozen fillies on your personal list right now," he persisted.

"Oh, I don't know . . ." Turrin sobered, then grinned suddenly. "A guy can go ape at first, if he don't use some will power. And that's bad. You either start to lose your appreciation, or you start to lose your head. And *that* is *real* bad. Sometimes a girl is referred over from one of the other operations. In those cases, I take a personal interest, get her logged into the computer, that sort of thing, you know. That's outside the regular recruiting channels. Sometimes I'll take a personal interest in the kid, help her get off with her best cheek forward, you know what I mean." Bolan knew what he meant, and a muscle twitched in his cheek. Turrin was not looking at his companion, however. "But I don't get into no entanglements," he continued. "Know what I mean? You can't get emotionally straddled with these girls. You know what I mean?"

Bolan nodded. "I think so," he said curtly.

"Besides, these girls getting fifty to a hundred bucks a toss get to thinking they got a gold-plated ass or something. I don't really like 'em. When I feel like cutting up a little, I go down to one o' my houses."

"You have those, too," Bolan observed wryly.

"Oh, sure. Really, I understand that end of things a lot better." Turrin grinned. "I *like* it better. That end is run entirely different. We got a madam for each house, just like the olden times. She runs her own books. We keep her supplied in girls, she runs the house, runs her own books, and feeds the money back in to the field man in her district. She works on commission, too, just like the field man, and he gets an override on everything she makes."

"Sounds like very big business," Bolan commented.

"You'll find out just how big," Turrin replied, "if you stick close to your C.O. Listen, we got ten women who do nothing but recruit girls. And you'd be surprised where we get some of them from. College campuses, factories, office buildings—" He raised his eyebrows. "—suburban *homes*—one gal we took on last month had just come off her honeymoon. We got chorus girls, models, would-be actresses and even some part-timers who really *are* actresses. Listen, every woman who *is* a woman has got at least a little whorin' streak in her. A lot of our call girls are part-timers. You know—they do other things, too. *All* of our party girls are part-timers, moonlighters. Hell, some of 'em wouldn't say '*fuck*' if they was getting gang-banged. Nicey-nice, you know—but not too damn nice to pick up some extra coin here'n there." Turrin frowned. "For *my* part, I'll take the good old honest whore. Well—" He paused, frowning even deeper. "You'll go outta your mind with the turnover we got in this business, Sarge. Understand something, and make sure you understand it. We have no competition in this town. Or anywhere around. If a girl is selling it within fifty miles of where you're standing, then she's selling for the organization and she's working for *me*. We—"

"I'm glad I understand that," the executioner said brusquely.

"Yeah—well, we don't even allow no amateurs to operate. We bust 'em fast, damn fast—and they either join our team or they get the hell out. That means we gotta fill the demand if we don't want a big payroll of nothing but broad-busters. I mean, there's no profit in that sort of thing. You understand that. I want you to understand me too, Sarge. I might not talk Yale or Harvard, but I'm a businessman and I know my business and I run my business all the way. Understand? All the way. No loose gooses around here, and just because I'm a good guy *some* of the time don't mean I'm an idiot. You better understand that. And just because I *like* you don't mean I won't *bust* you if you get outta line. You got that understanding?"

"I have that understanding."

"All right. You understand this, too. It's more profitable to keep the demand filled than to run around bustin' amateurs and chiselers. We got the high class hotels and motels pretty well covered with our computer call girl services, and we even got a few high class clubs and dining rooms as clients. But we got walking girls, too—we call 'em field girls. They operate strictly free-lance, some of 'em using their own pad as home base, and we trust 'em to play their finances square with us. We spot-check from time to time, but generally we use the honor system with the walking girls. They cover the little bars and clubs and some of 'em even serve as house girls for the crummy little hotels. We let 'em operate and we give 'em the protection of the organization. But they all belong to us. Understand that. Every damn one of them. Get the picture?"

"I get it," Bolan assured him.

"We treat our girls good. No strong-arm stuff as long as they keep in line. And we don't try to own 'em. They want to get out, they get out—but once out, they stay out, and they all know that. They're working for theirselves, see, and they all know that too. The organization does all their contact work—'cept for the field girls—and they get our full protection. *And* they keep the heavy share of the take. Like I told you, we're a democracy for the bold and the brave."

"Yeah, I remember," said Bolan the Bold.

"All right, come on," Turrin said, suddenly smiling. "I'm going to show you one of our house operations."

"I was wondering when we'd get around to the girl-watching," Bolan replied.

"You don't know what girl-watching is yet," the vice-lord of Pittsfield said chummily. "Come on, I'm taking you to my home away from home. I keep it stocked with the best stuff in Pittsfield, and I dare you to keep your eyes on and your hands off. And you gotta do just that. You gotta do *just* that."

8—Goddamn Iron-Man Bolan

It was a large house in the suburbs—nothing overly elaborate from the outside view, and certainly nothing to cause it to stand out from the other irregularly placed estates on the tree-lined street. An iron gate stood open, allowing ready access to the macadam drive. A gardener worked quietly in a flower bed near the front of the acreage of neat lawn. Numerous trees and shrubs dotted the landscape, all but hiding the house from street observation. A six-foot iron fence completed the isolation, there being no gate other than the automobile gate at the drive. Bolan looked again at the "gardener," deciding he was too young, too alert, and too near the open gate to be anything other than a disguised guard. Turrin brought the front wheels of the convertible to a temporary rest upon a slight lateral ridge in the driveway macadam, counting to five under his breath, then grinned at Bolan and gunned on along the curving drive toward the house. "We're up tight," he muttered. "There's a pressure switch buried in that hump. Always give it a five-second count, or you'll panic everybody in there." He nodded his head toward the white-painted structure looming in front of them. "We call the place 'Pinechester.' And it's legally chartered as a private club."

"Looks nice, but deserted," Bolan commented.

"Little early," Turrin grunted. "Don't get much daylight business. Most of the girls sleep until late afternoon, 'less they wanta get in some sunbathing or swimming or something." He noted Bolan's raised eyebrows, and added, "Yeah, there's a pool around back, nice one. This is one of our higher class houses. It's my pet, really. The girls here all treat me nice. They wanta stay here. Sheer luxury, huh."

Bolan had to agree. They passed a double tennis court and a golf-putting green. "How many girls?" he wanted to know.

"There's twenty-two bedrooms," Turrin replied proudly. "Sometimes we have more girls than that, sort of rotate days off and get the most out of the property. Real businesslike, you know." He glanced at his companion. "We sell memberships to this place. Like I said, it's a club. *Run* like a club. But the membership fee just gets the member in the door. Or he can use the pool and the other outdoors stuff at no extra charge. Then every so often we throw a party—by printed invitation *only*—and that costs the guy a *bundle*. We always got a waiting list for our parties." He pulled the car into a five-stall garage, killed the motor, and turned to Bolan with a huge grin. "We got half the aldermen in Gwinett on our party list. And the other half *trying* to get on," he added, chuckling.

They went in through a side door, and Bolan found himself standing ankle-deep in the carpeting of a wide hallway. "Library in here," Turrin announced, rapping lightly on the wall as they proceeded centerward. "Looks nice, but wasted space. Couple of thousand books in there just turning to dust."

They entered a smartly furnished room with a vaulted ceiling and two enormous crystal chandeliers. Couches and overstuffed chairs were placed here and there, in threesomes and foursomes, with accompanying side-tables, ash trays, and various bric-a-brac. "This's the clubroom," Turrin told him. "We tried to cozy it up some. It's a God-awful big room, and cozying wasn't easy." He tugged at an ornately woven pull cord. Bolan heard soft chimes echoing somewhere in the quieted mansion. A statuesque woman with flaming red hair piled high, empress fashion, strode into the room, a warm greeting on her lips.

"Leo dar-ling!" she cried happily. She ran to him and

embraced him, pulling back immediately to look warmly into his eyes. Bolan noted that she was a half-head taller than her employer, then took into account the impossibly high heels of her shoes and mentally calculated her back down to Leo's general height. She wore silk skin-tight hip-huggers that clung to her every suggestion, from belly button to ankles, and Bolan allowed that there was quite a bit of suggestion there. A silk jacket completed her attire. It had flaring, slitted sleeves, nicely exposing the rich skin tones of her arms as she moved them, and ended several inches above the waistband of the pants. The front of the jacket did not come together—three scarlet ties were provided as closures, but only one, squarely at bustline, was being employed. The gap at the center was a span of inches, and the ties no bulkier than a shoestring. The effect was startling, and found an interested audience in Mack Bolan. The redhead ignored him completely until Turrin made note of his presence.

"I want you to meet my new top-kick, Rheeda," he said. "Mack Bolan, Rheeda Devish."

The redhead looked him over then, and it was done in a single flash of interested eyes—yet Bolan had the uncomfortable feeling of being completely invaded in that brief inspection. She smiled and said, "Hi, Mack. How's the weather up there?"

"Warm," he replied, grinning.

"Oh, it's the environment," she said soberly. "Once you get acclimatized I'll have to get to know you better."

Bolan was unsure of the ground, but there was no mistaking the invitation of that friendly declaration. He wondered, but only briefly, about the degree of quote emotional involvement unquote between the girl and Turrin.

"And I guarantee you'll never be the same again,"

Turrin added quickly, chuckling, and removing the wonder from Bolan's mind.

"I can hardly wait," he replied, staring into warm, violet eyes. He felt a shiver at his spine, and hoped it was not observable from the outside. He had never known that women such as this one were to be found in the oldest profession.

"You'll have to," Turrin said, still chuckling. "Remember what I told you. All eyes, no hands." He moved his head closer. "Look, Sarge, Rheeda and I have business together. You're on station right here. Understand? Right here."

Bolan nodded soberly. "I'm on station, Captain."

Turrin winked and clapped Bolan on the shoulder. "God *damn*, I'm glad we found you, Sarge," he said warmly. Then he turned back to his redhead and together they left, going out the back archway and up padded stairs, the woman clinging in lock-step and giggling delightedly over something Turrin was saying to her.

Bolan shrugged his shoulders and paced about the big room, gazing at the paintings adorning the walls and wondering idly who had posed for the nude studies hanging everywhere. He decided that if the models were also residents of Pinechester then there was quite a world of prostitution he'd never been exposed to. The clubroom itself was sumptuous. He wondered if the bedrooms were equally lavish in devotion to the details of animal comforts—and decided that they probably were. The place reeked of luxurious flesh-pampering, which meant money with a capital "M," and Bolan wondered how much it did cost the monied American aristocracy for a night's indulgence in the pleasure palace. He could almost appreciate the grim satisfaction of a Sicilian "Matthew" peasant who had risen to the proprietorship of such a magnificent "cunt castle," as Turrin had referred to it, and who could so gladsomely relieve the rich of some of their riches and pass them on to some of the *nouveau riche* now luxuriating in the twenty-karat comfort of the suburban estate. Bolan pulled himself out of the thoughts, shaking them off, telling himself that Turrin was a hood, purely and simply a hood, a conscienceless goon who seduced little girls into prostitution and squeezed hard-working family men into desperate acts of violence.

Such were his thoughts when the blonde appeared, and she jarred every trickle of sanity from his suddenly shrieking synapses. She was fully as tall as Rheeda and made up in vibrant youth and oozing sex what Rheeda took from her in poise and beauty. The golden hair fell in a torrential sheen to below the creamy shoulders, reappearing in a loosely braided effect with the tail draped casually across the back of the neck and down onto the throat in a light curl. The eyes were widely spaced and sparkling blue, the nose and chin delicately chiseled, the jawline soft and barely defined. The richly sensuous mouth was provocatively ajar, the pink top of a tongue thoughtfully extended onto the upper lip.

"Who the heck are you?" she inquired in a soft voice.

"I'm waiting for Mr. Turrin," Mack told her. It seemed an idiot thing to say but, under the circumstances, it seemed also quite apropos. The golden goddess was, for all practical effects, unclothed. A transparent gauzelike stole was draped across her shoulders and in a free fall down the front of her, crossing at the arch of her thighs and drawn under, back, and around and tied loosely at the hips. The effect was altogether casual and altogether revealing and, in the altogether, stunning to male awareness. Huge globular breasts with strongly defined areolae surged restlessly beneath the gauzy film, scarlet tips only emphasized by the luminously white material. The soft midsection and soaring hips dramatically back-dropped the obviously darker shading of the swollen Mount of Venus, hardly more than accented by the transparent bow overlacing. The legs and thighs seemed to explode upwards with no loss of continuity between that below and that above, and Bolan found himself nervously wetting his lips like a schoolboy at his first strip show.

The blonde was regarding him studiously, getting his measure, and obviously approving of what she saw. She hooked curled fingers of both hands into the vee formed by the crisscross of material and slowly tracked the upward route, enlarging the open area of fleshy display. Bolan the unshakeable lost command of his eyes as the rubied tips jerked free and bounded toward him.

"You may as well wait upstairs with me," the blonde said, obviously sure of her effect on the straining male consciousness. "You may as well," she repeated coaxingly, in a husky voice. "Leo always takes about an hour. C'mon. We'll get a drink and take it upstairs."

"I'm sorry," Bolan said, already wondering about the genuineness of the encounter. "He told me to wait right here."

She moved against him then, and the delicate scents of her edged stronger into the male of him. His hands automatically moved onto the soft roundness behind her, then twitched away as the magic of chemistry had its way. She tossed her hips in a recognition signal, her lips nuzzling toward his ear, and whispered, "He always takes at least an hour. I'll bet it wouldn't take us five minutes."

Bolan politely but firmly pushed her away. "I'm sorry," he said quietly.

She gazed at him for a moment, reading the message of his eyes. Her own eyes flashed, then, and she asked, "Who do you think you're kidding?" Her nostrils were flaring angrily. "That's a roaring monster you've got there and you're just dying to bury it in me!"

"You are absolutely right," he replied agreeably.

The girl gave a short, nervous laugh, wriggled her

hips, and threw a vicious bump in his direction. "Picture it buried in *that!*" she cried.

"I got the picture," Bolan said. He grinned feebly. "Take it easy, blondie. This may be the place, but it just isn't the time. Now you haul that hot ass away from here and leave a working man alone."

Her eyes softened and she gazed at him with new respect. She said, "Well-l-l . . ." in a voice tinged with indecision, then simply smiled at him.

An electronic squeal and then a hum broke the silence, followed swiftly by the voice of Leo Turrin, obviously issuing from a concealed speaker somewhere in the clubroom. "Okay, Sarge," it said. "Another point for you. Hey, what are you? A goddamn iron man? Huh? I wonder if *I* could pass that test!" Turrin was enjoying himself and the moment hugely. "Hey—hey—grab that hot blonde and drag her delectable ass up the stairs. You hear me? Go on and enjoy yourself!"

"I hear you, Leo," Bolan said softly. He was looking for the speaker.

"Hey, it's closed-circuit TV. I'll show it to you later. Mitzi—you take good care of my friend—you hear me?"

The girl was smiling good-humoredly. "Sure, I hear you, Leo," she replied.

"And that makes another piece you owe me on the house!" He laughed uproariously. The speaker squealed, then was silent.

"See what your devotion to duty cost me?" the blonde said, now smiling ruefully at Bolan. She snared one of his hands and tugged at him. "Well, c'mon, let's go find some place to bury that bone. Or are you still saying it's not the time?"

"It's the time," Bolan agreed, moving in-tow toward the carpeted stairway. Bolan the goddamn iron man knew very well he could pass the next test—over, and over, and over again. He followed the blonde seductress up the curving sweep of stairs, along a wide, beautifully decorated hall, and into a large bedroom. It was a sumptuous affair, complete with canopied bed, deep carpeting, and lavish furnishings. Bolan emitted a soft whistle.

"Nice, eh," the blonde said, turning to him with a warm smile. Her gaze angled down to his loins, one hand moving spontaneously with the eyes. "What's your druthers?" she asked, lashes lowering demurely.

"What?" Bolan said, one hand toying with a soft shoulder.

"Do you prefer it sitting, standing, laying down, all-fours, belly-to-belly, or oral-genital?"

Bolan merely grinned, pushed her an arm's length away, and carefully untied the bow at her hips, thoughtfully disentangled the stole from the warm flesh of the thighs, drew it over her head, and dropped it to the floor, then stood gazing at her, one hand raised contemplatively to his chin. She smiled and did a slow pirouette, arms raised gracefully, concluding with a repetition of the bump-and-grind she had shown him downstairs.

"Don't tell me," he said, grinning, "—I'll bet you were on the stage."

She gave a short laugh, lowering her arms and standing somewhat awkwardly, perhaps even self-consciously. Bolan had taken command; this was obvious. She laughed again, a bit nervously, turned and strolled toward the bed, hesitating momentarily to gaze at him over her shoulder, then studiously folded back the bedcovers and crawled onto the luxury of silken sheets, plumping a pillow beneath her head and rolling languidly onto one side and staring at her companion of the boudoir. Bolan was undressing. She watched him as he stripped, her eyes following each flexure of the manly frame. He carefully draped his clothing over the back of a chair, stalked over to the bed, and stared down at her with a penetrating gaze, his lips set in a half-smile.

She smiled back at him and patted the bed beside her.

Bolan seized the patting hand and dragged her off the bed. She stumbled to her feet, spluttering. "You like to throw it," he said. "So throw it."

"Aw look, I was just—"

"Throw it!"

She threw it, repeatedly, grinding and tossing her hips in a pretty fair facsimile of a burlesque queen, and obviously tiring fast. Bolan was standing back, hands on hips, watching her labors. Presently she said, "Is this how you get your kicks or is this a grudge fight?" She had come to a panting halt, glaring at Bolan with a despairing light in her eyes. He laughed and folded her into a tight embrace, his flesh all but shrieking under the duress of the delightful head-to-toe contact.

"Let's just say that you passed *your* test," he told her, grinning down at her. "Now—how do *you* want it?"

She giggled and relaxed against him. "If I have a choice, I'll take it flat on my back and breathing slow."

"Okay," he said agreeably, "—at least we've got the display-window starch out of you."

"What?" She had fallen back onto the bed, tiredly drawing her legs onto the edge.

"All that posturing and posing," Bolan explained. "You put that on for all your callers?"

"I never get any complaints," she assured him.

He dropped his knees to the floor and encircled the lush female body with an arm, raking his lips across the torso, pausing momentarily at the breasts, then onto the throat and lingering on the pouting lips. "This is more like it," she said a moment later, sighing and running hands along his back. He doubled one of her legs and drew it forward, kissed the knee, kneading the leg and thigh with both hands.

"You, uh, like legs?" she asked, a new light beginning in the depths of her eyes.

"I like yours," he told her. "But probably not in the

way you're wondering. I'm just trying to discover where you tick."

"Hell, I tick all over," she said quickly. His hands had moved onto her hips, fanning along the heavy cones of firm flesh, and up into the juncture of legs and body. The raised leg jerked involuntarily and she inhaled sharply. He was grinning at her. "Well, okay, so I tick some places better than others," she admitted. "Are you going to, uh, get up here on the bed with me?"

For reply he pushed, pulled, and rolled her over and ran his hands along the back of her, hesitating here and there to probe sensitive spots. The blonde was beginning to puff again. "Say," she said, "say . . ."

"Yeah?"

She lunged about and flung her arms about his neck, mouth eagerly seeking his. He went onto the bed then and they lay in tight embrace, limbs intertwined, mouths joined, her hips moving rhythmically against him.

He withdrew from the urgency of her mouth and said, "Now, that's the proper movement for the bed set."

"Okay, Professor," she puffed, "—on with the lecture." Her mouth again grafted onto his, the heavy globes of breasts worrying frantically against his chest. Both hands came down off his neck and moved between them, searching, grasping.

He evaded her, saying, "I haven't seen your steam yet."

"God, God—how much steam you want a girl to have? I'm going nuts all over."

He rolled to the other side of her, carrying her over atop him, lifting her high, head beneath her chin, and buried his mouth in the luxurious flesh. She gasped and flopped, hammering at him with her hips, whining, entreating. Some moments later he pushed her onto her back and rolled off the bed to stand beside it and gaze down at her. Her knees and arms lifted together and her eyes were pleading. "Please," she moaned, "please . . ."

Bolan smiled approvingly, murmured, "Now you're a woman," and fell onto her.

She arched up to meet him, capturing him in a death-grip with all four limbs. "Yes, yes, yes," she panted, then her midsection exploded in a convulsive grasping, and it was not until some moments later that she was able to complete the statement. "I am a woman," she declared languidly.

"Hell, don't I know it," Bolan said tiredly.

All tests were A-OK.

BOOK TWO:

1—The Cause

An unexpected caller presented himself at the door of Mack Bolan's Liberty District apartment in the early morning hours of August 31st. Bolan grunted with surprise, swung the door open, and admitted Detective-Lieutenant Al Weatherbee. The see-all cop's eyes made a fast appraisal of the expensive lodging, then settled onto the slightly exasperated tenant.

"Consider this a friendship call," the policeman said, smiling tightly. "I want—"

"Five in the morning is a bit too early for friendship," Bolan observed.

"A friend in need doesn't know the time of day," Weatherbee advised him. "I just dropped by to pass along an interesting piece of information."

Bolan was not being a gracious host. He left the lieutenant standing in the center of the living room and went back to the small kitchen. He put a pot of water on the stove, pulled two cups and a jar of instant coffee from a shelf, then turned sleepy eyes toward the front of the apartment. "Come on back here," he called.

The huge bulk of the detective moved into the narrow dining compartment. Bolan was perched on a high stool at the breakfast bar. "Coffee be ready in a minute," he announced in a thick voice. "What'd you say about some information?"

Weatherbee nodded. "Came by way of an informant." He settled tenuously onto a stool, sitting sideways and studying Bolan's face in the dim light. "A contract has been let on you, Bolan."

Bolan thought about it for a moment, then said, "I don't understand you."

"A kill contract," the policeman explained. "Somebody has set *you* up for an execution. Understand now?"

Bolan stared at him briefly, lit a cigarette, and glanced toward the pot of water. Why does it take water so much longer to boil in the morning?" he asked soberly.

"You do know what I'm saying?"

"Yeah, I know." Bolan slid off the stool and stepped to the stove, touched the pot experimentally with fingertips, then angled a pentrating gaze toward his companion of the early morning. "You trying to shake me up, or something?" he asked softly.

Weatherbee sighed and shook his head negative. "No, this is on the level, Bolan. Look, I've had you under observation. I've known that you've been playing some sort of game with these people. Well—now *they* know it. You didn't really expect to insult their intelligence forever, did you?"

Bolan dug a spoon into the coffee jar, extracted a heaping spoonful, and slid the jar toward Weatherbee. "You're speaking of the Matthews," he declared. The water pot was just beginning to sizzle. Bolan glared at it, then lifted it off the stove and poured hot water into his cup, swizzling the coffee crystals mechanically with one hand while pouring water into his visitor's cup with the other. "They haven't seemed so intelligent," he murmured.

"Many, many dead men have had that same first impression," Weatherbee said. He stirred his coffee and took an experimental sip. "They've pegged you, Bolan," he declared, exhaling noisily. "They know who you are —and obviously they know why you are interested in them. And there's a contract out, with your name on it."

"What can I do about it?" Bolan wondered aloud.

Their eyes met. Weatherbee smiled grimly and said:

"Run. As fast and as far as you can. Southeast Asia, if you can get there."

Bolan shook his head. "I'm not running anywhere. How long has this, uh, contract been in effect?"

Weatherbee glanced at his watch. "About four hours, if my informant's information is accurate."

"And how long does it take them to get something going?"

Weatherbee shrugged the massive shoulders. "Not long. They must figure it as a fairly easy hit. The price on the contract, I'm told, is only five thousand." He sighed. "To tell the truth, Bolan, I rather half expected to find you already dead when I came up here."

"Why all the intrigue?" Bolan wanted to know. "I've been under their noses for days. Why the cat and mouse routine? They could have taken me any time."

"Why yours?"

"Huh?"

The big cop smiled. "Why have you been holding off? Your object is to kill them—and don't bother denying or confirming that, I don't expect you to. It's a matter of *modus operandi*, isn't it. The same is true of the Mafia. Contract killings are their way." He pushed the coffee away from him with a grunt. "The coffee is lousy. You didn't let the water boil. Well . . ." He got down off the stool, placed his hands on his hips and rocked back, stretching himself. ". . . I've told you. That's my duty, as I see it. It's all I can do, unless you want to request protective custody."

Bolan's reaction to the suggestion was a disparaging grunt. "Where do I stand legally? If I kill them first?" he asked.

"You'd be arrested and charged with first degree murder," Weatherbee replied calmly. He was walking toward the front door.

Bolan stalked him through the apartment. "It would be self-defense," he pointed out.

"You'd have to prove that in court," the policeman informed him. He paused at the door and turned back with a taut smile. "Look, if it means anything—you have my sympathy. But that's entirely unofficial. If you exercise that trigger finger once more in this town I'll be right on top of you, and that's the way it has to be. Now I'd say that you're between the devil and the deep deep blue. I advise, first of all, that you admit to the killings of August twenty-second and surrender yourself. A good lawyer just might be able to build a good case on temporary insanity. If you don't like that advice, then I can only say *run*. Run like hell. You can't fight these people, Bolan. You just can't fight them." He opened the door and stepped into the hallway. "Well—you want to get dressed and go with me?"

Bolan shook his head, said, "Thanks, Lieutenant" and closed the door. He went immediately to the bathroom, calmly brushed his teeth, then shaved, showered, and dressed. He examined the flip-out shoulder holster which had been provided by Turrin, inspected the snub-nosed pistol for the dozenth time, then slipped into the harness and secured it. Next he went to the kitchen and took four boxes of ammunition from a drawer, emptied the boxes, and redistributed the ammo for the .32 loosely into his pockets. Then he returned to the bedroom and rearranged the furniture, sliding the head of the bed against the east window, opened the blinds at that window to admit the strong rays of the rising sun, loosely rolled the blankets into soft lumps and pulled a sheet over them. He went through the apartment, then, carefully closing all blinds and extinguishing lamps, returning finally to the bedroom.

He positioned a chair inside the walk-in closet, went over and closed the bedroom door firmly, then returned to the closet and sat down, rolling the sliding doors to a faintly cracked closure directly in front of the chair, checked the .32 one last time, then waited with a calm and patience he had learned in another part of the world.

The second visitation to the Bolan apartment on the morning of August 31st occurred at just a few minutes before seven o'clock. This time the visitors were two in number, and they did not ring the bell. They stood in the hallway for a moment, ears pressed to the door of the Bolan apartment, while one of them fussed with a mechanical gadget of sliding blades and protruding prongs. He tried several combinations on the door, moving with quiet care, then whispered, "Think I got it." The door swung softly open. The two men paused momentarily, then stepped quietly into the apartment, closing the door carefully behind them. The interior was not entirely darkened but they stood quietly by the door for a moment allowing their eyes to adjust to the gray gloom.

"Still in bed," one hissed.

The other nodded silently and they moved slowly toward the rear of the apartment. The larger man paused near the bedroom door, squinting in the near dark to inspect a long-barrel pistol he held in his hand. A silencing device was attached to the barrel of the pistol. The other man touched the pistol, his teeth revealing themselves in a smile. "No pissin' around," he whispered. "This guy's good with a gun, they say."

The man with the pistol nodded and slowly turned the knob of the bedroom door, pushed the door wide, and stepped inside, the second man right behind. They were momentarily blinded, squinting into the bright rectangle of sunlight beyond the bed, but the gunman raised his arm and squeezed off three quick shots into the huddled lump on the bed, the big pistol "plutting" dully under the muzzle silencer. Then there was a sliding sound in the corner to their right and a voice announced, "Over here, Charlie."

The two men spun as one, arms almost interlocking. Orange flame was spitting toward them and the room was vibrating with the testimony of a fast-talking pistol. A scarlet geyser erupted from the throat of the man with the gun. The other crumpled to his knees, one hand inside his jacket and frozen in a Napoleonic imitation, the jacket itself quickly turning crimson directly over the heart. Another projectile punched into the first man's face, just beneath one eye, the impact snapping his head back grotesquely. He went down atop his companion, the thoroughly silenced pistol clutched spasmodically in an uncontrollably jerking hand.

The Executioner stepped out of the closet and stood over them momentarily to confirm the results with a professional eye, then holstered his gun and quickly left the apartment. He took the elevator to the basement, then hurried up the stairway of the rear service entrance to the building, crossed the alleyway, fitted a key into the service door to the opposite building, and went in. A minute or so later he entered a small apartment of that building and went to a hotplate and started some water for coffee. Then he removed the cushions from a couch and produced a high-powered rifle. The .444 Marlin sported a very businesslike telescope sight; the metal parts of the rifle were wrapped in a protective gauze. A metal ammunition box and a cleaning kit appeared from beneath the couch, and The Executioner began methodically preparing his tools for service.

"*Who* is insulting *whose* intelligence?" he muttered. To anyone who might have been interested, sniper-expert Bolan could have explained that every planned offensive also contained an avenue of retreat. "This's no retreat, though," he told the Marlin, unfolding it affectionately from its gauze covering. "It's just a tactical withdrawal to a holding position." He walked to the window and gazed onto the street below. A siren was sounding from not far away. He wondered how The Matthews would feel when they learned that the contract was still wide open. He wondered, also, how Lieutenant Weatherbee would greet the news. The Executioner, he realized, would have to step with exceeding caution from this point onward. Everybody would be after him now—the cops, the Mafia, the contract killers, probably the whole damn world. Bolan shivered slightly.

Fear is a natural emotion, he told himself. *Use it! Make it work for you!* It was a pep talk he had used many times before. But then, he had never been completely alone before. *Make it work for you!* Of course! Scare the shit out of The Matthews. Get them running scared, keep them more scared than you are, and hope that they come unglued. But how do you handle cops? the Mafia wide open, get them running scared, evade them. How long could he evade them? Not long, he was realist enough to understand that fact. He had, probably, a few days at the most. A few days. Well—he'd have to do what he had to do in a few days. He had to crack the Mafia wide open, get them running scared, evade their killers, evade the cops, and keep himself from coming unglued in the process—all in a matter of two or three days. Could he do it? He patted the big Marlin. Well—he'd do it or die. It was that simple. A chill chased down his spine. It was as simple as that.

Bolan discovered a truth in that stark moment of self-confrontation. He had started this thing as an act of simple vengeance. He could face that truth now. A strong sense of justice, a galvanic feeling of frustration, and a willingness to undertake independent action—these three had conspired to spell vengeance for Mack Bolan. But vengeance was no longer the issue, nor was self-defense, and this was another realization of Bolan's new truth. He no longer hated these people, these Matthews, as exemplified by Turrin, Plasky, and Seymour. He had almost learned to understand them and, in so doing, had found his hatred melting. He had come to regard them now in almost the same way he had learned to think of the enemy in Vietnam.

There was nothing personal between Bolan and the enemy, no hatred, no score to settle. Life was just an overgrown game of cowboys and Indians. There were good guys, and there were bad guys. The bad guys had to lose. It was as simple as that. The Executioner had come to realize that he was fighting a holy war, corny as it sounded. Good over evil, this was the issue. This was the cause, and Executioner Bolan knew that he would never find a better one to live for. To *live* for—not to *die* for. There was no victory in dying, this was so clear to him; the victory lay only in the death of evil, and Mack Bolan found himself irreversibly committed to that undertaking. The Mafia was evil. The Mafia must die. This was the cause.

2—The Rattler

It was just a little past noon when the familiar black sedan pulled slowly through the iron gateway to the suburban estate, the front wheels pausing briefly on a raised lump in the driveway. The driver of the sedan nodded to the young man in the caretaker's overalls and moved the car smoothly along the curving drive of Pinechester. He wheeled on around to the garage area, left the vehicle, and entered the large house through the side door, going directly to the pullcord in the clubroom, announcing his presence. After a small wait, the tall redhead appeared, again sporting silken hip-huggers, these of a flaming green and slitted strategically for ultimate effect. The tailored smile faded from the pretty face. "S-sarge," she stuttered, eyes quickly flicking beyond him in search of another presence. "Wh-what . . . ?"

"What am I doing here?" he finished the question for her, smiling. "Can't you guess?"

The professional smile immediately reasserted itself. She laughed nervously and took a hesitant step toward him. "Mitzi told me you're a devil," she said, her voice rising in obvious discomfort. "I suppose you—you've come to tame *me* this time, eh? Okay." She swayed forward, hands moving toward his neck.

He stepped back and batted her hands down. "You know better than that," he told her.

"What do you want?" she asked, now obviously frightened.

"I want you to get your girls out of here," he told her, "—unless you want them toasted like marshmallows."

She stared at him uncomprehendingly for a brief moment. "Is the house on fire?" she mumbled.

"It's going to be," he assured her. "Start getting them out. Now!"

Her eyes flared angrily, then wavered under the unrelenting impact of the Bolan gaze, and she spun about uncertainly, then went quickly to a small desk near the doorway, opened a drawer, and fumbled inside. Bolan the cat had moved silently behind her; he shoved her roughly and she fell into a nearby chair with a startled cry. She got hesitantly to her feet, rubbing a scraped wrist against the silken pants, glowering darkly at Bolan as he removed the clip from a tiny automatic pistol he had taken from the desk drawer.

"You better hurry," he told her mildly. "I'm putting the torch to this place in about thirty seconds. Take 'em down the fire escape in the back." He slung the automatic across the room, picked up a newspaper, and held it over the flame of his cigarette lighter. Rheeda gasped and bolted up the stairway.

Bolan tossed the flaming newspaper to the floor, beneath the window draperies, then quickly lit another. Moments later the clubroom was a blazing inferno. Bolan exited the same way he'd arrived, climbed into the car, and drove back to the gate. "The joint's on fire," he called to the "gardener." The man threw him a surprised look, then turned his gaze toward the house, reacted visibly, and immediately took off on a hard run for the flaming structure.

"These old places do go up fast," Bolan muttered to himself, then he grinned and pulled on through the gateway and drove up the road, paralleling the fence, for a distance of about a hundred yards. He pulled onto the shoulder, stopped the car, then carefully eased it alongside the fence and killed the motor. He reached into the back seat and produced the big Marlin, then left the car and scaled the fence, dropping lightly inside with the rifle slung over his shoulder. Smiling grimly, he crossed the grounds to a small knoll overlooking the house and drive, lay down, and again took up a patient vigil.

Women were shrieking and running about, most of them in various stages of undress. Bolan could easily spot the flaming green of Rheeda's outfit. He sighted her in with the scope and her angry face leaped into the field of vision. Bolan grinned. Rheeda was fit to be tied. The old structure was consumed in flames already. The "gardener" was moving slowly among the women, talking animatedly, a large revolver inanely clasped in one hand. The distant scream of fire trucks edged into Bolan's consciousness and a Chief's car flashed into the driveway moments later, executed a quick circle on the lawn, and bounced to a halt just inside the gate. A uniformed man jumped from the car and waved down the hook and ladder truck entering just behind him, passed some brief instructions, then stepped back and allowed the truck to proceed on toward the house. Bolan grinned again. Telling them to never-mind the hoses, he guessed. The place would be gutted before they could even get the hoses laid out. Rheeda and the women were now clustered about the truck. The firemen seemed to be showing more attention to the girls than to the blaze. Another truck was turned back at the gate by the Chief, who then returned to his car and drove on to the house.

Bolan grinned and waited. There was an explosion down in the fire, followed closely by another. Bolan supposed that nobody had thought to move the cars from the garage. The generally unclad women were beginning to move about restlessly, and one barefoot young lady in a nightgown was trudging along the driveway toward the road. *Getting worried*, Bolan decided. He could understand why. Some embarrassing questions would likely be raised concerning the presence of so many underdressed young women on the premises.

A police car turned into the drive, stopped and picked up the deserter, then proceeded to the group on the lawn. Bolan could see Rheeda talking to the cop. He sighted them in, studying the faces. Old friends, obviously. The cop was grinning and nodding his head in response to something Rheeda was telling him.

The firemen were watching the house burn to the ground. Most of the young women were sitting on the lawn. Rheeda and two others were in the police car. The Fire Chief was leaning against the patrol cruiser watching the young women. A limousine pulled into the gateway, inched forward, as though from force of habit, and rested front wheels on the macadam hump. Bolan already had the occupants sighted in. Turrin sat on the passenger's side, in front. The man behind the wheel he recognized as one of the "guns" of Seymour's poolside party. Two other men, their faces not visible to Bolan, were in the back seat.

Bolan shot the front tires off the car as they rested on the hump, then put a quick round through the windshield between the two men. Turrin's startled and frightened face passed swiftly through the scope viewer as he hit the deck. A back door swung open and a large man staggered onto the drive, one hand held to a bleeding scratch at the side of his head. Bolan clucked his tongue; he had not meant to hit any flesh on that first salvo. The sounds of the big rifle boomed across the open ground. The policeman leaped from his car and started toward the fire; all attention in that area was directed to the roaring inferno. Bolan chuckled and swung once again onto the car in the gateway. The driver was trying to move the car on shattered tires. Bolan put an imaginary mark on the hood, under which the carburetor should rest, and levered two quick shots into there. The car stopped moving immediately; the hood blew open and resettled at a skewed angle, and flames licked up around the opening. All doors popped open and galvanized men erupted from the car and sprinted for the cover of the trees a few yards distant. Bolan had been expecting it;

he punched a .444 through one man's leg and let it go at that, swinging about to scope in the police car. The cop was tugging at his holstered gun and running toward the burning car in the gateway. The confusion around the firesite was working to Bolan's advantage, this much was obvious; as yet, no one had connected the knoll with the gunshots. He decided to use the confusion while he could, and punched two shots down onto the police car, dropping two of its wheels onto the ground. The women vacated rapidly, darting about in panic while the Fire Chief's car settled onto two of its rims.

Bolan then slung the rifle at his shoulder and slid down the backside of the knoll, deciding that he had rattled enough teeth for the moment. He had to climb a tree to overcome the fence, dropping onto the roof of the car. He carefully stowed the Marlin, climbed behind the wheel and swung the car in a U-turn across the road, then cruised slowly past the scene of excitement he had just vacated. He caught a glimpse of the policeman, gun in hand and a baffled look on his face, staring at the remains of the wrecked limousine. The car's occupants were nowhere in sight. Curious sightseers were beginning to descend upon the scene, and already several cars were pulled over along the shoulder of the road. Bolan gunned on past the entrance to the estate, a satisfied smile on his face, and set course for the home of Leo Turrin, some eight miles distant in another suburban area.

He covered the distance in something under twenty minutes, arriving at Turrin's front door at precisely two o'clock. A pretty, dark-haired woman of about thirty answered his ring. She responded with a warm smile when Bolan introduced himself, and invited him in. He declined, preferring to deliver his message while standing in the doorway.

"My name is familiar to you, then?" he asked her.

"Oh, yes," she assured him. "Leo has spoken very

highly of you, Mr. Bolan. Are you sure you wouldn't like to come in? I don't know when—"

"No, I really didn't expect to find Leo here," Bolan said quickly. "As a matter of fact, I just left him a little while ago. I neglected to tell him something important—and I was in the area—I thought I could leave the message with you."

"Do I need a pad and pencil?" she inquired, smiling brightly.

"No, it's a simple message," Bolan replied soberly. "Tell him that the iron man broke the contract, and that I would have returned it to him at the fire this afternoon, but that I figured he could wait another day or two."

"I—I guess I have that," she said, gazing at Bolan curiously.

"Fine. And please remind him that I could have just as easily returned it to his wife and children." Bolan smiled. "That part is important also. Please don't forget it."

The pretty brunette's face had clouded. "Mr. Bolan, I—I don't . . ."

"It's sort of a code," he said. "Leo will understand the meaning."

"I see," she replied. Bolan had turned and was heading down the steps. She followed. "Uh—Mr. Bolan—if you will forgive my forwardness—just what is your relationship with my husband?"

He turned to her with a pleasant smile. "Hasn't he told you? Don't you know what your husband's business is, Mrs. Turrin?"

"Well, yes, of course." A vague cloud of doubt seemed to momentarily eclipse the light in her eyes. Bolan guessed the eclipse had been there many times before. "But he has so many interests. I was—just—wondering . . ."

"Where I fit in?" Bolan finished the question for her.

She nodded, her face a mixture of curiosity and embarrassment.

Bolan hated to hit her with it. She seemed a very nice person. But there were overriding considerations. "I'm one of his guns."

"What?"

Bolan casually opened his jacket and let her see the .32 snuggling into his armpit. "Didn't you know that your husband is a Mafiosi?" he asked calmly.

"A *what?*" She practically screamed it, her face twisted into a stiff mask of shock and horror.

"I'm sure there's enough Latin in your veins to figure that out, Mrs. Turrin," Bolan said cordially. He moved on down the steps and into his car without looking back. She was still standing there in the doorway when he drove away, body rigid, hands raised to her face. Bolan felt like the biggest bastard in the world. It wasn't much fun rattling those kind of teeth. He sighed and headed the black sedan toward Walter Seymour's estate. Well, a rattle was a rattle. It was that sort of a war. Tomorrow that pretty woman would be a widow. And tonight she would have a very frightened husband on her hands. There was no morality in a holy war. It was simply a matter of ultimate good versus ultimate evil. It did not really matter that good becomes evil in the heat of the battle. Combat reduces everything to evil—life itself becomes an evil thing in the heat of the battle. How many times in bygone years had he threshed through these same old stale ideas? Why torture himself with mystical concepts of good and evil? The Mafia was evil. Any opposition to the Mafia is therefore good. The lines of battle were clearly drawn. The only morality in battle was to fight the good fight, to stand strong against the assault and to counterattack unfalteringly when the time was come. This was a soldier's morality. Mack Bolan was a soldier's soldier. He glanced at his watch. If the traffic did not get too bad, he could make Seymour's place by three o'clock. This rattle would prove interesting indeed. Yes. Perhaps he would make it a death rattle. And perhaps the vibrations would make themselves felt throughout the inner circle, the high council, the family fathers. Perhaps he would rattle their house down.

3—Penetration

He stopped the car on a narrow dirt road to the rear of the Seymour estate, removed his jacket, and pulled on green coveralls. He unholstered the .32 and shoved it into the waistband of his trousers, then belted on a leather tool kit similar to the type worn by telephone and power company linemen. One of the compartments carried a broad-bladed hunting knife; there were also pliers, screwdrivers, cutting tools, and various other implements. A small mousset bag on a shoulder sling completed the outfit. Bolan left the Marlin in the car, walked through a wooded lot, and easily breached the redwood fence to the Seymour place through the simple expedient of wrenching loose several of the boards. Obviously Seymour placed more reliance on live security than on Maginot lines, and Bolan suspected that much of that live security had been drained off to the Pinechester crisis.

The place, indeed, appeared to be deserted. Walking boldly in the open, he made it to the swimming pool unchallenged, gazed about with almost fond memories, then produced a packet from the mousset bag, ripped it open, and tossed it into the pool. The water immediately began to take on a brilliant red coloration under the influence of the powerful marker-dye. He then kicked over two of the cabanas and shoved them into the pool. He watched them for a moment, wondering if they were going to float or sink, and had about decided on "float" when a man in white slacks and a red jacket jogged around the corner of hedgerow and onto the poolsite, his eyes flickering rapidly back and forth between Bolan and the pool.

"What th' hell?" the man growled. His hand went inside the jacket and returned with a pistol in tow.

Bolan ignored the pistol. "I dunno," he said calmly. "I think something's happened to your pool." His gaze was pure innocence; he turned his back on the security man to peer into the water. "Come and see for yourself," he suggested.

The man stepped up beside him, staring stupidly into the pool, the gun gripped tightly in front of him and pointed into the water. "I don't . . ." he started to say, the words eclipsing into a bloody bubble. The gun slipped into the pool and he raised surprised hands to a suddenly and unaccountably slit throat, then tumbled forward into the pool only a second or two behind the gun, the rush of blood hardly visible in the already stained waters. Bolan dropped to one knee and swished the blade of the hunting knife in the pool, then dried it, sighed, and sheathed it. The body had disappeared beneath the dye; Bolan rose and walked toward the house, his eyes raised and seeking power and phone cables. Locating them, he ambled casually to a rear corner of the house, pulled the insulated cutters from their holster, and deprived the Seymour home of telephone service, then moved a few feet further on and sliced through the main power cable.

There were immediate sounds of activity inside the house. A back door opened and a middle-aged woman emerged, rubbing her hands nervously on a gaily decorated apron. Her troubled gaze swept over Bolan, then she grunted and said, "Well, what is it now?"

"Doing some work on the lines, ma'am," Bolan said, smiling apologetically.

"Well, you picked a swinging time," she told him, obviously chafing with exasperation. "I'm trying to fix dinner. How long's it going to be off?"

Bolan ignored the question; another gun had pushed excitedly through the doorway. "Everything's off," he growled, the ever-present pistol dangling in a relaxed grip.

"What's the gun for?" Bolan asked, then quipped: "You going to shoot me for losing your lights?"

The man glared at him, but reholstered the gun. "How long they gonna be off?" he asked, his tone surly and complaining.

"If I can get a couple guys to help me. I'll have them back on in a jiffy," Bolan told him.

The man jerked his head in an impatient nod. "I'll help," he said. "What do we—?"

"I need two men," Bolan insisted.

"There's another guy out here somewhere. We'll—"

"I've got him doing something else," Bolan persisted. "I need—"

"Well, that's tough shit!" the gunman roared. "There's nobody else around! Get your own goddamn—!"

"Okay, okay . . ." Bolan took him by the arm and walked him toward the pool. The cook was moving back inside. "I guess we can handle it ourselves," Bolan was saying chattily. "Trouble's down here by the pool. See, the—"

They had rounded the corner of the poolside patio, and the gunman was reacting visibly to the confrontation. "Well, shit, what's happened here?" he cried.

"Electron storm, see," Bolan was saying, straight-faced. "Inductance from the pool into the power cables, see. Come here, I'll show you." He had stepped to the side of the pool, and was peering into the water.

The security man moved slowly to join him, the gun hand sliding softly toward the armpit. He stood beside The Executioner, one hand raised to the back of his neck, eyes roving unbelievingly across the red waters and onto the floating cabanas.

"Electrons are powerful little demons," Bolan said soberly. "The power of the atom, you know."

"I still don't get it," the gunman mumbled. The hand

had found the comforting contour of the pistol grip and was slowly moving into the open. Bolan's hand had been busy also. The hunting knife whipped up and over, slicing across veins, arteries, and tendons of the gun hand. The man gave a startled grunt and jerked hastily away, but the long flat blade had already found another mark deep in his abdomen and was now slicing back toward the surface in a twisting withdrawal. Bolan's other hand, at the man's back, pushed gently and the scarlet waters accommodated another visitor.

Bolan cleaned the blade once again, muttered, "There's no morality in a holy war," and returned to the house.

The cook met him at the back door. "They're still off," she complained.

"Should be okay now," Bolan told her. "I'd better come inside and take a look."

She nodded and stepped aside. Bolan went in and gazed around the kitchen. "Smell that?" he asked her.

"Just my pot roast," she replied uneasily.

"No—there's something wrong in here," he assured her. "You'd better go outside—get clear away from the house."

She nodded her head in quick agreement and stepped toward the door.

"Is anybody else in the house?"

She shook her head negatively and hurried outside. Bolan moved swiftly then, on through the kitchen and past the dining room and up the stairs to the upper level. He unsheathed the hunting knife and went from bedroom to bedroom, slashing every mattress in the house from head to foot, a task requiring less than two minutes. Returning through the living room, he noted a large portrait of Walt Seymour hanging over the mantel. Bolan coolly sighted his .32 and emptied it into the portrait, completely punching out both eyes. Then he reloaded the pistol, returned it to the waistband of his trousers, and rejoined the cook on the back lawn.

"I heard explosions!" she cried excitedly.

"Yes, ma'am," Bolan said. He walked on past her without another word.

She scampered along after him. "Should I call the fire department?" she asked breathlessly.

"No, ma'am," he said, turning back to gaze at her reflectively. "Uh—you're not a member of the family, are you?"

She shook her head. "I just work here," she cried shrilly.

"Then I suggest you find a job somewhere else, and quick."

"Why?"

"Because your employer does not have long to live, that's why. You tell him that." Bolan dug into the mousset bag, located a metallic object, and pressed it into the woman's hand.

"What's this?" she asked, eyes clouding in confusion.

"You give that to Mr. Seymour. Tell him it's from The Executioner. Tell him it will be just this easy when his time comes. Just this easy. You understand that?"

She nodded vaguely, holding the object up to view it better. "My son got one of these," she said dully. "It's a marksman's badge or something."

"Yes, ma'am. You just give that to Mr. Seymour, and give him my message."

"You're not from the power company," she said, the realization just dawning on her.

"No, ma'am. The house is safe enough if you want to go back in." Bolan left her standing there and reversed his route across the grounds, through the fence, and back to the car. He returned the tool kit and coveralls to the trunk compartment, climbed in behind the wheel, lit a cigarette, and inspected his hands for steadiness. They were shaking a little. It was okay, he realized, it was the proper time to shake. He started the engine and moved the car slowly along the dirt road. He would have enjoyed hanging around and watching Seymour's reaction to The Executioner's penetration of the defense perimeter—but there would be another time for that. *If* time did not run out for The Executioner. There would be a great hue and cry now, that much was certain. The newspapers would certainly get in on the act; no doubt pressures would be brought to bear on the police. A madman was running loose in Pittsfield. Bolan grinned and gunned the sedan up a little incline and onto a paved highway. A madman with a cause. The important thing was that the House of Mafia would be vibrating from basement to attic. He had shown them how vulnerable they were. The battle would be joined and it would get personal, highly personal. It would not be a matter of cold-blooded murder contracts; this would be a war of emotion, and fear, and the constant threat of sudden death. It was Bolan's kind of war. It was the kind of warfare in which he was an expert. The Matthews would surely recognize that fact now. They'd been penetrated, and they'd damn well know it.

4—The Understanding

Bolan stopped at a public telephone, thumbed a dime into the slot, and dialed the number for the central police station. "Lieutenant Weatherbee, Homicide," he told the switchboard operator. He waited, humming softly under his breath, until the familiar drawl of the detective came on the line.

"Weatherbee here."

"Bolan here."

"Oh? Where, uh, where you calling from, Bolan?"

"Forget the intrigue, Lieutenant," Bolan advised. "I just wanted to let you know that contract's still open."

"Yeah, uh, you've been busy busy busy, haven't you."

Bolan chuckled. "They yelling?" he asked.

"At the very limit of their lungs, that's all. There's a warrant for you. Arson, assault, assault with intent, attempted murder—shall I go on?"

"Naw, save it," Bolan suggested. "There'll be a lot more to add before the day is done."

The detective's tone was plainly troubled. "Why'd you call, Bolan?"

"I want to ask a favor."

"Oh? You want to turn yourself in? That's about the best favor I can offer—the lockup."

Bolan was chuckling. "Not hardly. I'd like for you to move my brother into the police ward at the hospital."

"Oh, I did that early this morning."

"Very thoughtful of you," Bolan said, his voice revealing his surprise.

"Yeah, I think of a lot of things," the cop told him. "Like—you've really managed to isolate yourself from the world, haven't you."

"Maybe."

"Maybe, hell. You've torn it good, Sergeant. Everybody wants you now, even the military. CID men just left here."

"You sure lost no time calling *them* in." Bolan was plainly miffed.

"Uh-uh, not me. Somebody with political influence blew the whistle, no doubt. They're running scared, Bolan."

"You don't sound too mad at me."

"I'm not. I'm tickled to death. Unofficially, of course. Also unofficially there's a lot of people down here rooting for you. Don't expect any official sympathy, though. As far as the law's concerned, Bolan, you're just as rotten as the best of them—and let me assure you . . . uh, just a minute . . ."

Bolan could hear the vague rumble of background voices, then the Lieutenant was back on the line. "You been out in the Portal area lately?" he asked, the voice somewhat brisker.

"Could be."

"Near the home of a Walter Seymour?"

"Maybe."

"Uh-huh. Well . . ." More background noises, then: "You can add two counts of first-degree murder to that warrant. You'd better come on in now, Bolan. This thing has gone far enough."

"Not nearly."

"Huh?"

"Not nearly far enough. It's unconditional warfare, Weatherbee. You may as well understand that. And listen. Don't send any plainclothes cops in my direction. I'll shoot anything that moves against me, unless I can clearly identify the law."

"You wouldn't shoot a cop, eh?"

"I'd rather not. Well—I have a crowded schedule, better bug off. I've enjoyed the chat."

"Bolan—that informant I was telling you about . . ."

"Yeah?"

"He's on my other line right now. Like to hear some more interesting information?"

Bolan chuckled. "I love gossip."

Weatherbee cleared his throat heavily. "You may not love this tidbit. That contract has been expanded. Not ten minutes ago. It is now open season on one Mack-the-Knife Bolan, with every hood in the East joining the game. You are now worth a hundred gee's, dead in the street, buddy. How do you like them apples?"

"So, they *are* running scared."

"You dumb bastard, can't you see what you've done? You're attracting every gunsel in ten states into our town."

"That's exactly what I want," Bolan clipped back. "Now you cops are going to have to move off the side-lines, aren't you."

"Bolan, you're a lunatic! You—"

"I'm a catalyst, Lieutenant! I've smoked a ratpack out from under their cover of respectability—and now you're going to have to do something about them, aren't you!"

The detective's angry voice rattled the telephone receiver. "We're going to do something about you too, Bolan."

"So we understand each other," The Executioner replied levelly.

"Yeah, we understand each other. But Bolan . . ."

"I'm still here."

"Don't shoot a cop."

"I'd rather not."

"You'd better not! Like I said, you've got some unofficial sympathy down here right now, but . . ."

"We understand each other," Bolan clipped. He hung up, grinning, and returned to the car. A glance at his watch informed him that the time was 4:40. He would just about have time to make it over to the Triangle office. His smile broadened and he started the engine and eased into the rush-hour traffic. He thought of Weatherbee and chuckled, feeling a bit sorry for the serious-minded cop. It was good to understand people, Bolan decided. Understandings were highly important in warfare. They were, indeed, all-important. And now, Bolan needed to cement an understanding with the Mafia—a financial understanding. He angled into a turn-lane and headed directly for the loan company.

5—A Gut Transaction

Bolan stepped through the door at five minutes before five o'clock, closed it firmly and locked it, and pulled down the shade. The girl at the reception desk showed him a startled attention, and Bolan showed her the little plastic-embossed card supplied by Turrin. "You're closed for the day," he snapped. His eyes flicked toward the closed door beyond the plastic and wood interview cages. "Who's in there?" he asked harshly.

"J-just Mr. T-thomas," the girl stammered.

Another girl popped up behind a wire enclosure. Bolan turned his attention immediately upon her. "Are you the cashier?" he asked her.

"Yes, sir," she replied breathlessly.

"Got your day's accounts in order?"

She nodded. "Yes, sir, just now."

Bolan was moving around behind the cage. "Bundle everything up and take it into Thomas' office, the money too, everything." He pulled the receptionist to her feet and gently pushed her toward the back office. "Get in there and call Thomas to get his books ready for a spot audit. Everything on the top of the desk, please." He was rattling the wire gate to the cashier's cage. "Let me in there, I'll give you a hand," he barked.

The receptionist turned back to him with a pained expression. "I—I forgot your name," she said.

"Just tell him I'm from Plasky's office," he snapped. "Move—move! I don't have all night!"

The girl nodded and half-ran across the outer office, rapped lightly on the closed door, and swept inside. Bolan picked up a wooden tray and began stacking currency the cashier was removing from her cash drawer.

The two of them noisily invaded the private office a

moment later. Thomas, the office manager, scowled at Bolan and said, "I don't think—"

"Good, don't think," Bolan snapped him off. "You haven't been here long enough to start thinking." He jerked a thumb toward a massive steel door. "Get the vault open," he commanded.

The young man's face was showing an inner conflict. "I'd like to see your, uh, identification," he said.

Bolan once again swept the plastic card into sight, held it briefly in front of the man's eyes, then returned it to his pocket. He smiled suddenly, a warm reach of friendship. "Look, don't be so nervous," he said softly. "Plasky thinks these spot audits will keep you on your toes. You have nothing to worry about, I'm sure. Open the vault so we can get this over with."

Thomas hesitatingly began working the combination of the door lock, then turned the big wheel and swung the door open. "What is your cash on hand?" Bolan asked tersely.

The cashier thrust a scrap of paper tape into the manager's hand. He glanced at it. "Forty-two thousand, six hundred eighty-nine and forty," he mumbled.

"Oh Goddamn, not *that* figure," Bolan replied with obvious exasperation. "The *holding* fund, Thomas, damnit, not your nickels and dimes."

The younger man blinked, stepped into the vault, slid back a section of steel wall, and produced a large leather case. "Why didn't you say so in the first place," he complained petulantly.

"Open it," Bolan commanded.

Thomas fished a key from somewhere inside the vault, inserted it into the case lock, then blinked past Bolan to the young women who were standing awkwardly in the center of the office floor. Bolan understood the look.

"You ladies wait in the outer office," he said. The two girls exchanged glances and went out. Thomas carried the case over to his desk, opened it, and glared at Bolan.

"I hope to God you don't want to count it," he said miserably.

"What's the tally?"

"Two hundred and fifty thousand."

"Certified?"

The manager nodded and produced a sheet of paper from the top of the stacked currency. Bolan pretended to study the list of figures, said, "Uh-huh," and moved back toward the vault.

"Just exactly what are you looking for?" Thomas wanted to know.

"Come here and I'll show you," Bolan said. He jerked the other man inside the vault and slammed his head against the steel wall. The young man's legs rubberized and he slid to the floor. Bolan stepped past him and began hurling ledgers and records out into the office. He stripped the vault completely, stuffing currency into the open case on the manager's desk and piling everything else on the floor. He slammed and locked the vault door, then touched his lighter to the pile of papers on the floor, picked up the case of money, and went out to join the young ladies.

"I want all your records out here—out here on the floor," he barked. The girls looked at each other, then began opening drawers and arranging papers and file folders atop the counter. "Don't be so dainty about it," Bolan said roughly. "This's an emergency." He swept the records to the floor, then went over to a metal file cabinet and began unloading the drawers. Minutes later a bonfire was raging in the outer office, and the eyes of the young ladies were beginning to reflect the presence of a madman in their midst.

Bolan seized the cashier and pressed a marksman's medal into her hand. "Tell Plasky The Executioner said it was easy as pie," he said calmly.

"Wh-what?"

"Just tell him that. Oh, and you'd better go get that

guy out of the vault before this whole place goes up. Oh, and tell Plasky thanks for the bucks, they'll come in handy." He picked up the case of money and opened the door. The girls were already dashing toward the private office. Bolan chuckled and stepped onto the sidewalk, pulling the door firmly closed. He'd returned to the scene of the crime, and by God he'd committed another one, and by God he wondered how The Family would appreciate this one. He suspected that financial considerations were gut-matters to the Matthews. Bolan suspected also that he certainly knew how to hurt a *Mafiosi.* He walked around the corner, got into his car, and chuckled all the way home.

6—The Council

"Listen, something's gotta be done about that sonuvabitch!" Seymour snarled. "He's running wild, hog wild, all over the damn place—burning, and killing, and stealing, and—and . . ."

"Look who's complaining," Turrin commented bitterly.

"Yes, I'm complaining!" Seymour roared. "He was *your* goddamn man! Couldn't you spot the son of a bitch for a phoney without having to get word down from upstairs? You creep, you bastard you—Jesus Christ, any dumb dago wop would know the son of a bitch is a phoney! If you weren't laying up with those fucking sluts of yours all the goddamn time you might—"

Turrin leaped to his feet and threw a wild punch at his tormentor. Seymour dodged back out of the way, his face going white, his hand scrabbling about for a weapon and coming up with a Coke bottle.

Nat Plasky stepped between them, his arms waving wildly. "Stop it! Stop it!" he yelled. "Don't you think this is what the bastard wants? He wants us at each other's throats. Now stop it!"

Leo Turrin's lips were quivering with rage, but he hunched his shoulders, clenched his hands together, and dropped back into his chair.

"I'm sorry, Leo," Seymour said humbly. "I didn't mean that crack about the wops."

Turrin merely nodded and stared broodingly at the toe of his shoe.

"The Man is going to be very upset over that quarter-million," Plasky said, after a short silence.

Seymour nodded his head. "We'll get it back."

"Sure we will," Turrin sneered mildly.

"I don't hardly remember even what the guy looks

like," Plasky ventured. "I only saw him twice, and then just for a few minutes. How the hell did he know about the organization money being in that vault? Huh? How'd he know?"

"Didn't you know?" Turrin grunted. "He's the fuckin' Phantom. The fuckin' Phantom knows everything."

"I thought that was the Shadow," Plasky mused.

"Will you two for Christ's sake shut up!" Seymour roared.

"Just passin' the time," Plasky replied meekly.

"Well, crack your knuckles or something," Seymour growled. He studied his watch for a moment. "The others will be here in a few minutes."

Turrin heaved up out of his chair and went over to the bar, half-filled a tumbler with bourbon, added an ice cube, then carried it back to his chair, sipping glumly. "The trouble," Turrin said presently, "is that you people don't know this guy. I do. I know him. And I'm shakin'. Believe me, I'm shakin'. This guy is a military machine, believe me. I had a sergeant like him once, just about like him. He scared the shit outta me, too. And so does Bolan. I'm telling you, this guy—"

"Damnit, shut up!" Seymour screamed emotionally.

"No, no I'm not gonna shut up," Turrin went on stubbornly. "You gotta know who you're dealing with. Now look at it, just look at it. The *nerve* of this bastard. In the space of—what—three or four hours?—he hits us bing! bing! bing!—just like clockwork. He burns down my prize palace, completely wrecks an eight-thousand dollar automobile, scares the living shit right outta me, smashes Jake's leg, completely terrorizes and demolishes the whole damn place—" He paused to sip nervously at his drink. "—then he slips away and turns up a few minutes later at *my house—my* house, mind you, has a chatty little ratfink conversation with my wife, and God that's a whole 'nother story—" He laughed nervously. "—then, pow! he shows up at Seymour's shack, dyes the swimming pool red, tosses in a couple of bath houses and the carved-up bodies of Paul and Tony, cuts off the phones and lights, slashes up the beds—just to show us what could've happened if somebody had been in them, I guess—and unloads five slugs into Walt's fancy oil painting. Now—that should be enough to hold anybody for a week—but no—he ain't done yet. He cruises down to Triangle, burns all the loan records, locks Thomas in the vault, and walks away with a quarter-million of our buried bucks. I had a sergeant like that once. He took it into his head to screw every whore in Singapore, without paying yet, and he damn near did."

"Are you now finished with your eulogy?" Seymour asked coldly.

"Yeah. I'm finished. And I think we oughta suggest to the council that we all blow this town for a while. We all need a vacation anyway. I been promising the wife I'd take her to Acapulco for a swing. Let the contract boys take over, and we can come home after it's all settled."

Plasky laughed nervously. Seymour was glaring at Turrin with cold contempt. At that moment the double doors were swept open and four men entered, forming a sort of honor guard for an older man who walked in between them. The three men already present rose quickly to their feet. The four-man guard force deployed themselves about the room, one remaining in the open doorway. The fifth, a man of about 60 with white hair and a kindly face, shook hands with the other three, his warm eyes and firm grasp reassuring them. He took his place at the head of the table.

"Well, now, what is going on, eh?" he asked mildly, his eyes shifting from Seymour to Plasky to Turrin and back to Seymour again.

"It's this nut, Bolan," Seymour replied in a choked voice. "The hit didn't go off. I guess he got the drop on the two boys from Philadelphia. Anyway, he got them instead."

"Yes, I know about that," the white-haired man said calmly.

"Well, now he's gone berserk," Plasky put in. "He's been making hits all over town. He hit my operation and walked away with the bag-drop—a quarter of a million dollars."

"He burned down my prize palace and terrorized my wife," Turrin said, staring at his fingers.

"He killed two of my boys," Seymour groused. "Raised hell with my house, too."

"Raised hell?"

Seymour nodded. "Put dye in my pool. Destroyed two cabanas. Cut through the power cable and the telephone line. Slashed up all of my beds." He shrugged. "I'd call that raising hell."

"Shot up his oil painting, too," Turrin added with a half-smile. "You know the fancy one over the mantel, the Chairman of the Board type picture."

"Is this one soldier, or is this one army?" the man asked, raising his eyebrows.

"It's one lunatic!" Seymour said savagely. "Listen, Sergio, we got to *do* something about this nut!"

"So what have you been doing?" the one called Sergio inquired.

The three men exchanged embarrassed glances.

"Besides hiding, I mean." The old man coughed delicately. "Has the organization grown so soft? So soft that one man, one lone man, can send the entire organization scampering into holes?"

"This's no ordinary man," Turrin said defensively. "I had a sergeant once that—"

"Oh for God's sake shut up about your goddamn whore-hopping sergeant!" Seymour cried.

Turrin jumped to his feet and shook his fist at the other. "One more word outta you about my whores and

I'm gonna shove one right square up your ass, Mr. Comptroller—you understand? Right up your ass!"

"Sit down and shut up, Leopold!" Sergio snapped. "Why take out all your anger on one another? There is a common enemy—is there not?" He shook a finger at Walt Seymour. "And all this is your ultimate responsibility, Walter," he added. "Can you see this? The first mistake was yours. You let him in, and gave him the opportunity to know us. Can you see this? And now the advantage is his. He can go to the ground now and dare us to sniff him out. This is costing a lot of money, a lot of money."

"I suspected him right from the start," Seymour growled. "Plasky's the one brought him in. I figured he was some sort of plant. I've just been waiting for him to hang himself."

"You dumb shit!" Turrin snarled. "Who the hell do you think he's hanging? Himself?"

"*Shut up!*" the old man roared, showing his fire. "The dumbnesses have been done and they are finished. Understand? They are finished! One more, just one more, and we will bring The Family together in full council and some dumbnesses will end up in the river! Do you understand? Do you?"

"Yes, Sergio," Turrin replied meekly.

"Well?" The old man's eyes were blazing full glare on the other two.

"Sure—sure, Sergio," Seymour said quickly.

"I understand, Sergio," Plasky assured him.

"Twenty years ago I would not sit at the same table with such rabbits," the old man said scathingly. "All right, listen to me. I have issued the open contract on your Bolan. But you cannot rest behind that. Now you have money, you have brains, you have power, and you are *Mafiosi!* Now why should Sergio care about this Bolan—eh? Is Bolan after Sergio? No. No. Bolan is after Walter, and Nathan, and Leopold. Eh? Bolan does not even know of Sergio. Right?" He snapped his fingers at one of the background men and made a drinking motion with his other hand. The man swung around to the bar, poured a glass of wine, and moved quickly to the table with it, placing it before the old man. He sipped it. The others remained silent. The man who had brought the wine went back to his station. Sergio sipped again, then placed the glass on the table. "Just the same," the old man continued, "Sergio has put one hundred thousand dollars on the line for your necks. The *Family* cares, you see. Just see that you are deserving of that care. Eh?"

At that instant the picture-window at the far side of the room seemed to explode and fall apart. The man who had just served Sergio grunted and fell forward onto his face. The glass containing the wine disappeared, but the wine remained to form a pool on the surface of the table. The delayed *cra-ack* of a high-powered rifle galvanized the paralyzed men at the table, the four of them taking to the floor beneath the table, their faces contorted with the fear of a personal doomsday. The distant explosions were rolling in unceasingly now and the *thwack* of big-calibre bullets plowing into floors and walls told eloquently the story of cause and effect.

The fusillade ended as abruptly as it had begun. Turrin raised his head and stared into the frightened eyes of the white-haired Sergio. Plasky and Seymour were grunting with emotion. The four other men were strewn about the large room in crumpled heaps.

"He knows you now, Father Sergio," Turrin declared shakily.

The old lips curled back over dully gleaming teeth and a balled fist pounded impotently upon the floor. "Get him!" Sergio hissed. "Get this Bolan! You understand? *Get this Bolan!*"

7—The Goof

It was time to be moving on to another billet. The Executioner could not afford to spend too much time in any one spot. He had changed into night-fighter garb of dull black. The .32 calibre pistol had been replaced by a .45 calibre U.S. Army automatic, strapped to his waist. He wore black sneakers and a black beret. He looked at himself in a mirror and laughed. The tight-fitting costume gave him a comic-strip appearance. If he should bump into anyone on the street, they'd probably think him dressed for a masquerade ball. The Marlin and the case of Mafia money were already stowed in the car, along with other personal effects. He went through the small apartment one last time to be sure that there was no evidence of his habitation there, then picked up the bag and departed. It was twenty minutes past two o'clock in the morning. He drove directly to Leo Turrin's home, arriving there at a few minutes before three. It was a fashionable district of curving streets and upper middle-class homes. Bolan left his car on a street behind the Turrin place, vaulted a fence, and cut across another piece of property to reach the Turrin rear approach. A dog began barking several yards down. Bolan climbed atop Turrin's garage and lay on the dark side of the sloping roof, studying the house for interior layout. A dim light burned behind a frosted window downstairs, obviously a bathroom. Another faint glow was issuing from a room upstairs. Bolan remembered that there were three Turrin children, and tried to sketch in bedroom details in his mind. The upstairs glow, he decided, was coming from a nursery or at least a child's bedroom. Again he tried to project the interior arrangement of the home into his mind, but the outside architecture was too unusual to provide any reliable clues to the inner structure. The windows appeared to be of the type which crank open, and all in Bolan's vision were closed tightly.

Somebody had come out and quieted the barking dog. Bolan thought about that for a moment, then looked around for something to make some noise with. He pried loose a Spanish tile from the peak of the garage roof and hurled it to the patio below. It struck a metal table with a loud clank then slithered across the flagstones with great effect. Bolan's eyes were straining in the effort to cover all windows at once. He was rewarded. A drapery moved, in a window of a corner upstairs. Somebody was peering out of the window, but this was more a feeling than a certainty. He pried off another tile and repeated the performance. The drapery swung with sudden motion and a light came on in the same room. Bolan caught a glimpse of Leo Turrin hastily turning away from the window and, before the drape could swing closed, a momentary exposé of a dark-haired woman upon a bed, her hand still upon a lamp at bedside. Bolan grinned, imagining Turrin's consternation when his wife roused and switched on that lamp. He lay still, waited, and watched—and again was rewarded. Turrin, in pajamas, was out in the yard, inching along in the shadows of the house. Apparently he had come out the front door and was making a flanking movement around the side of the house. Bolan smiled appreciatively, and watched. Turrin was at the back corner now, standing very still. Undoubtedly he was armed. They played the waiting game for several minutes, then something sailed across the patio and bounced against the side of the garage. Bolan smiled. Same game, same rules, he thought. Then he lost sight of the prey. He lay still and waited, eyes probing the darkness, thankful for his advantage of height. He was aware, also, of another advantage. A woman and three children, flesh and blood of the adversary, were within that house—a pressure point for the interloper. Bolan wondered vaguely why Turrin had not evacuated the civilians, but there was no time to push on for a decision on the question. Turrin had reappeared at the far corner, apparently reversing his field with a probe to the other flank.

Bolan was once again beginning to respect the Sicilian. At least he was out there, in the open, taking the battle to the enemy, not in there hiding with the women and children. He moved into the open then and said, "Bolan?" in a soft voice. Bolan shook his head and silently clucked his tongue. Turrin was walking toward the garage, very slowly, stopping every couple of steps and pausing momentarily, apparently to listen. There was a gun in his hand, Bolan could see it plainly now. A flashlight was in the other. Bolan considered that for a moment, and watched Turrin pass by the garage and move on to the other side of the yard. Silently Bolan slithered down the sloping roof, dropped lightly to the ground, and boldly stepped off toward the shadows of the house. He heard Turrin's soft "Bolan?" once again, coming from the far back corner of the property, then he moved quietly around the side of the house and up the steps to the front door. Just as he suspected, the door was standing slightly ajar. He grinned. There were obviously no pockets in Turrin's pajamas—and if he was carrying a gun in one hand and a flashlight in the other, it had been a lead-pipe cinch he wasn't carrying a housekey between his toes—he wouldn't have locked himself out. Bolan slipped inside the house and stood in the darkened entrance foyer, wondering how much longer Turrin would wander around out there in the yard. He really had not desired to kill Leo from a distance, with a sniper's bullet. There had been a certain friendship between them—the least Bolan could do was to look him in the eye as he killed him. Irrational, perhaps, he realized that, but then war itself was irrational. The wait was not a long one. Turrin came in only a minute or so behind

Bolan, breathing softly. He closed the door and locked it and stood there for a moment, his back to the unsuspected visitor. Bolan wondered about the thoughts occupying the mind of the prey as he stood there silently in the dark at that locked door—what was he thinking?—what were the last thoughts of a doomed man?

Bolan reached forward and placed the muzzle of the .45 at the base of Turrin's head. "I knew it," Turrin sighed, exhaling quickly. "I knew you were there the moment I turned that lock." There was a brief silence, then: "You don't want to shoot me, Bolan—not until we've talked it over."

"It will be a lousy mess for your wife to clean up," Bolan said quietly. The darkness was stygian, but Bolan could feel the mask of death twisting the other man's face. Bolan had seen it before, other places; he had worn it himself, many times, and knew how it felt, the grotesque twisting of all the little muscles awaiting the final clap of doom, the paralyzed diaphragm, the aching ribcage. He did not want to prolong that misery. His free hand reached forward.

"Let go the gun, Leo," he commanded. The long-barreled pistol reluctantly changed hands. Bolan tossed it behind him and it clattered to the floor.

"I can't blame you for the way you feel," Turrin said, his voice tight with emotion.

"You can't?"

"No. Your sister was a sweet kid, Bolan."

"You just said the wrong thing, mister," Bolan said savagely, jabbing the automatic harshly into the unyielding skull. "Now unlock that door and open it, slowly—*slowly!*"

"Where we going?" Turrin asked, half-choking on the words.

"A tender mercy for the wife and kids," Bolan said harshly.

At that instant an overhead light flashed into brilliance. Bolan reacted automatically, flinging himself sideways against the wall, the .45 swinging up and around, seeking a new threat. Turrin's wife stood several feet inside the living room, her face a terrified mask, one hand raised and stretched toward Bolan. He checked the heavy swing of the .45 just in time, his shot gouging into a chair and sending it skittering across the room. Bolan's eyes were smarting under the sudden candlepower and his ears rang from the boom of the heavy-calibre gun, magnified by the closeness of the foyer; perhaps this is why he did not see the tiny pistol in Angelina Turrin's outstretched hand. The little popping sounds it was making seemed to bear no relevance to the sudden stinging sensations at his shoulder and temple, but he knew instinctively that he had been shot. Turrin had flung himself away and down and was rolling madly across the floor. Bolan squeezed off two shots at the retreating figure as he lurched out the door, routed by a petite woman with a dainty weapon—not only routed but wounded in the process. He could feel the blood running down the side of his neck as he pounded around the corner of the house, and wondered vaguely how seriously he was hit. He got the .45 holstered on the run and cleared the fence without effort, and decided that he could not be hurt too badly although the shoulder was beginning to burn fiercely. He dashed across the other yard and was nearly into the street when he heard the sounds of converging sirens. He hesitated only for a moment, electing to leave the car sit where it was rather than to try outwitting the cops in an automobile at such an hour of the morning. Any car in motion would be a certain target for the cops. He ran on across the street and through another yard, then diagonally across an open field. Distance was what he needed right now—as much distance as he could get on foot and bleeding from two gunshot wounds. Well, he thought, you deserve it, you dumb bastard. He'd tried to fraternize with the enemy. It wouldn't work. Damnit, there was no such thing as morality in warfare. You drop them when you can and where you can. It is kill or be killed. He'd learned the lesson well in the jungles of Southeast Asia. Why had he chosen to forget it *here*, in the jungles of the Mafia? He cursed himself for an idiot and hurried on to a distant hulk of buildings, pressing his beret against the head wound to stanch the flow of blood. The entire world seemed alive with screaming sirens. The cops had been waiting for him, of course. They'd staked out his known targets and just sat back and waited for him to strike. Another mistake for The Executioner. He would have to reassess his battle plan. He wasn't going against the wily Cong now. He was going against the wily Americans, and he wasn't going to be allowed many mistakes like this one. And, judging from the roaring in his ears, perhaps he would not be allowed even this one. He was shot, and he was bleeding to death, and he knew it. He needed more than distance now. It was a mistake that he got shot, it shouldn't have turned out that way, but it did, and wars are lost on mistakes. He needed more than distance. He knew that. He needed a place to lay his head, a place to rest his wounds, a place to stuff back in the precious lifeblood. The Executioner needed a sanctuary. Or else the wrong person was going to end up being executed. It was as certain as death. The Executioner had goofed.

8—Sanctuary

A bleary-eyed Lieutenant Weatherbee stepped from the squad car and walked over to the police cruiser that was swung into the intersection just above the Turrin residence. He nodded tiredly at the uniformed cop who stood at the open door of the cruiser and said, "How soon after the gunshots did you get this street sealed?"

"Must have been less than a half-minute," the officer replied. "I was on station two blocks down. Soon's I heard the shooting I came right on up, and I've been here ever since. Only thing I've seen is our own people."

Weatherbee grunted, stared down the street for several seconds, then returned to his car. The plainclothesman behind the wheel gave him a sympathetic look. "Slipped through, didn't he," the man said quietly.

Weatherbee sighed. "I'm sure he did. Turrin says he was dressed like a commando, all in black. Said he moves as soft as a cat, and just about as fast. That Turrin is a mighty lucky boy, and doesn't he know it."

"You have to admire that Bolan guy," the officer commented.

"Maybe *you* have to." Weatherbee grunted. "*I* don't."

"Don't get me wrong, Al. I just meant—well, you know, he didn't even return the Turrin woman's fire. I mean, he could have taken her easy, we both know that. Instead, he elected to break off and run."

"Maybe he panicked," Weatherbee mused. "She thinks she hit him. Just because we couldn't find any blood . . . A wounded man isn't going to run too far, Bob. I'm going to get about twenty more men on foot in this area. I've got to stop that guy before . . ." He picked up the radio microphone and smoothly passed instructions over the special net, then he told his driver, "Okay, let's get over to the eastern perimeter and work back this way."

The man nodded, wheeled the squad car about and speeded eastward on the city arterial. "We shoot to kill, right?" the man said under his breath.

"You damn well better," Weatherbee replied glumly.

They turned onto a north-south residential street and immediately went into a slow cruise. Weatherbee released a short-barrelled shotgun from the rack and inspected it for readiness. The driver unholstered his revolver and placed it on the seat beside his leg. "Well, it's a lousy way to make a living," he muttered, sighing heavily.

"Hell, you're talking to an expert on the subject," Weatherbee said. "Look . . ." He stiffened suddenly. "Somebody just opened a door down there in those duplexes. Cut your lights!"

Bolan's legs were getting rubbery and each breath he took was becoming sheer misery. He had reached a more modest neighborhood and was painfully making his way across an open expanse of well-kept lawn bordering an apartment complex when he saw a window light up on a ground floor in the curving row of buildings. He dropped to one knee and examined the gauze pad he'd thrust in between his blouse and the shoulder wound. It was not bleeding quite so badly now, he decided—or maybe he was just running out of blood. He made a wry face and felt gingerly with fingertips the scratch at his temple. He'd lost a bit of skin on that one, and that was all, and the blood had started to clot pretty well, but it still hurt like hell and he had a headache that wouldn't quit.

He threw himself prone suddenly and rolled into a clump of hedges; automobile headlights had swept around the curve in the street downrange from Bolan's position and almost at the same instant a door had opened in a building slightly uprange. The headlamps winked out immediately and Bolan knew a sinking sensation as he noted that the car was still moving forward slowly in his direction. An outside light flashed on, up at the open door, and a woman stepped outside. She was wearing a housecoat and something was tied about her head. She was calling out something in a soft voice; to Bolan's exhausted consciousness it sounded as though she were whispering, "Titty, titty."

The automobile glided past within spitting distance of Bolan and stopped opposite the woman. She recoiled back toward her door and a man's voice, from the driver's window of the car, sang out briskly: "Police, lady. What's the trouble?"

Bolan could hear the woman catch her breath then giggle nervously. She walked halfway across the lawn toward the curb, remaining well within the glow from the porch light, then halted as the door on the opposite side of the car opened and a huge bulk of a man stepped out and addressed her over the top of the automobile. "I'm Lieutenant Weatherbee," he said genially, "We are looking for a man. Would you mind telling us what you are doing out here at this time of night?"

"Well, I'm not looking for a *man*," she replied, laughing breathlessly. "My cat woke me up yowling, and I thought I'd better bring her in. There's a big mean tomcat around here that just—"

"Yes, ma'am—well, there *is* a dangerous man in the area. We'd just better check it out." Weatherbee had moved around the rear of the car and was standing on the sidewalk, a shotgun cradled casually in one arm. The other officer got out of the car and was looking about nervously, peering into the darkened areas to either side of the building. The trio was near enough that Bolan could hear the woman's flustered breathing.

Weatherbee had requested permission to look inside the house, and the woman had consented. "Stay here with the young lady, Bob," the lieutenant said, and went cautiously down the walk and into the building.

The other officer had leaned inside the squad car and was now directing a spotlight along the sides of the buildings. Weatherbee reappeared, then went out of sight again in the shadows. Something brushed against Bolan's cheek; he checked his reaction in the flashing recognition of purring cat fur, and quietly curled his good arm about the animal and stroked it lovingly. The cat settled there in the crook of Bolan's arm, curled into a contented ball.

Weatherbee showed up again, walking into the brilliant spot of the police car light, stepped quickly out of it, and approached the couple at the curb in a tired amble. "Did you find my cat?" the woman asked.

"No, ma'am, nor mine." Weatherbee replied. "You'd better let the cat go for now. Go on back inside and lock your door. We will wait here until you're safely buttoned up. And thank you for your trouble."

The woman said something Bolan did not catch, laughed lightly, and ran to the door, turned and waved at the policemen, then went inside and closed the door. The porch light went out. A moment later the headlights of the police car flashed on and it moved on down the street.

Bolan clung to the cat and ran to the building in a low crouch, then harshly ruffled and pulled the cat's fur, holding it against the screen door. The cat screeched and clawed at the screen, fighting to loose itself from Bolan's grasp. Almost immediately the door cracked open. Bolan flung the screen door aside and stepped in, thrusting the cat into the arms of the stunned woman.

"I brought you your cat," he said, grinning. He closed the door and leaned against it. "Please don't raise a fuss. I'll leave if you insist."

She was looking at him as though it were all too unbelievable, and as though she expected him to vaporize or disappear into the thin air he had sprung from. Her eyes took in his weird costume, the gun at his waist, the blood-soaked shoulder. "You're hurt," she mumbled.

He nodded his head. "I've been shot. If you'll just let me stay a while I promise you won't be hurt." The shoulder was beginning to burn as though a hot poker had been stabbed into it.

"The policeman said you're dangerous," she said in a half-whisper.

"Not for you," he assured her.

The cat leaped from the woman's arms and ran into another room. Bolan gazed longingly at the couch. "There's a small bullet in my shoulder," he said. "I need some disinfectant and a pair of tweezers."

"Of course." She moved swiftly toward a narrow hallway. Bolan followed, not certain that she was not trying to get to a telephone. She stepped into a bathroom. He sighed, returned to the living room, and sank onto the couch.

"Do you live alone?" he called out tiredly.

Her head reappeared in the open bathroom doorway. "Nope. Tabatha lives with me." She wrinkled her nose. "Tabatha is my cat. Two old maids together, that's us." She went out of sight again, and Bolan began working his way out of the jersey blouse. When she returned to the living room carrying a small metal tray, Bolan had succeeded in freeing one arm and his head from the tight-fitting slipover and was carefully peeling it away from his injured arm. The woman had removed the scarf affair from her head and had obviously taken time to hastily brush out her hair from the large rollers it had been wrapped around. Bolan decided that she was a very pretty woman, small and delicate with luminous eyes and a decidedly intelligent face.

She set the tray on a coffee table and helped him with the blouse, making sympathetic sounds over the shoulder wound. "It's been bleeding a lot," she observed. "Is the bullet still in there?"

He nodded grimly, his eyes on the tray she had brought in. A pair of eyebrow tweezers stood upright in a small glass of colorless liquid. A roll of gauze, a box of bandages, and a large bottle of merthiolate completed the assortment.

"I'm sterilizing the tweezers in alcohol," she told him. "Is that all right?" He nodded his head again and reached for the merthiolate. "Do you expect me to take that bullet out?" she asked.

"No," he said. "I've done it before. I can do it again."

She pushed him over flat and moved a pillow beneath his head. "You're not going to do this one," she said firmly. She picked up the tweezers. "Now hold still," she said, between clenched teeth.

9—The Lull

Bolan was lying on a silk-draped lounge, naked from the waist down. Angelina Turrin, in revealing green hip-huggers, was sitting astride him, pressing a glowing soldering iron into his shoulder. "You're a goddamn iron man, Sarge," Leo said, from somewhere in the background, "—and that's a damn sweet little wife you got there."

"I'm going to kill you just the same," Bolan said calmly, "just as soon as I wake up."

He did awaken immediately, bright sunshine spilling into his eyes and little fire demons dancing inside his shoulder. A girl was standing at a window next to the bed, doing something to the venetian blinds, her back to him. Jet black hair cascaded onto delicately curved and bare shoulders; she was dressed in a bra and a half-slip, this fact causing her considerable embarrassment when she turned and saw that his eyes were open. She grabbed a smock from the foot of the bed, turned her back to him once again, and fumbled her way into the billowing garment.

"You're the cat lady," he said groggily.

She perched on the edge of the bed and shoved a thermometer into his mouth. "I thought you would sleep the day through," she told him, then shushed his reply with a meaningful glance at the thermometer. They looked at each other in silence for a while, eyes locked together, the girl smiling faintly. Then she retrieved the thermometer, studied it intently, and said: "Well, you must be an ox. Not a sign of a temperature."

"It's all in my shoulder, I think," he replied, grinning.

"I know who you are," she told him, her face going serious.

"Is it good or bad?" he asked, watching her eyes.

"Bad I guess," she said soberly. "It's all over television and radio and your picture is in the morning paper. They're calling you 'The Executioner.' Are you an executioner, Mr. Bolan?"

"Let me see, I'll bet you have a very exotic name," he said. "Carmencita. Yeah. You look like a Carmencita."

She flushed. "It's Valentina. Querente. You can call me Val."

"Valentina fits you better," he told her. "What time is it?"

"It's nearly noon."

"Which means you've had plenty of time to call the cops and get me off your hands. Why haven't you?"

"I almost did," she replied, peering at him from beneath partially lowered lashes.

"But you didn't. Why?"

"Well—you did trust me, didn't you? Besides—a man is innocent until proven guilty."

"I'm guilty as sin," he said.

"I know."

"Just how much do you know?"

"All of it, I guess. You've killed eleven men in less than two weeks. You're a living tragedy, Mr. Bolan. I suppose that is why I couldn't turn you in."

He smiled. "You sympathize with my cause, then?"

She shook her head firmly. "Not at all. No man has a right to take human life. There is never any justification for killing."

"No kidding?"

"No kidding. There's no way to justify it."

Bolan chuckled and shifted to a more comfortable position. "I don't need to justify it," he told her. "It justifies itself."

She moved another pillow over to offer better support to the wounded shoulder. "The end justifies the means?" she asked, smiling faintly.

"No—the means justify the end. It's the ages-old battle, Valentina. Good versus evil. Good justifies itself. Doesn't it?"

"I'll argue that with you some day," she said soberly. "—after we have identified *good.* Right now I'm going to get some food into you. How do you like your eggs?"

"Cooked," he said, grinning.

"Seriously."

"Seriously, I like them cooked. Any way you go about it. Uh—what happened to my clothes?"

She made a face. "I stole them. You picked on the wrong old maid, Mr. Bolan. When I get 'em in *my* bed, I *keep* 'em there."

"Some old maid," he replied, staring soberly into her eyes.

She colored and jumped to her feet. "Scrambled," she said.

"Huh?"

"No matter which way I go about it, they come out scrambled. So I hope you eat them that way." She smiled and sailed out of the room.

Bolan immediately threw back the covers and cautiously moved to the side of the bed. He was stark naked. He stared at himself for a moment, then regained the protection of the bedcovers. "What'd you say you did with my clothes?" he called.

"I said I stole 'em," she replied from the kitchen. "If you're going to be disagreeable about it, you can steal 'em back. In the bathroom, if you feel able."

Bolan felt able. He pushed to a sitting position and swung his feet over the side of the bed, fought back a wave of dizziness and got up and staggered nakedly to the bathroom. The black jerseys were pinned to a clothes hanger, suspended from the shower curtain rod. They had obviously been washed and drip-dried. The jockey shorts were on a towel rack, also clean and dry. He slipped into the shorts, grabbed the jerseys, and went back to sit on the side of the bed. Valentina rapped her knuckles lightly on the doorjamb and said, "Don't put the shirt on until I change the bandage."

"The way I feel under that bandage," he growled, "I may never put that shirt on."

"Are you decent?" she asked.

"I guess so," he replied.

She stepped into the room, stared at him frankly, and said, "Well, almost anyway. You'd better let me help you with those pants. Honestly, that is the most ridiculous outfit. Who do you think you are—Captain Marvel?" She was kneeling at his feet, and she seized the jersey pants and began stuffing his feet into them.

"They're entirely practical for sneaking about," he replied.

"I'll bet. Into your tent I'll creep, huh?"

Bolan was embarrassed, and he realized this with some surprise. "They, uh, really are very practical," he said. "The first time you try going over a fence or other obstacle in a baggy outfit you'll know what I mean."

"I know what you mean," she told him. She had threaded his legs into the costume to just above the knees. "I guess you'll have to manage the rest by yourself." she said. "I'll bet the eggs are burning up."

"You took 'em all the way off," Bolan observed pointedly. "Is there some reason why you can't put them all the way back on?"

"I said, the eggs are burning up." She went to the doorway, then threw him an impudent look. "Besides, I just skinned them off from beneath the covers and I didn't see a darned thing."

Bolan had his mouth open but she was already gone. He smiled and stood up and succeeded in finishing the job with his good hand. She was quite a gal, he was deciding, even if the unmistakable odor of burning eggs was drifting through the open doorway. Yeah, quite a gal.

The Sergio Frenchi home dominated the skyline of South Hills, the luxury suburb of Pittsfield. The site had been selected because of its resemblance to the Mediterranean coastline, though the ocean was hundreds of miles distant, and the house itself was of traditional Mediterranean architecture, stone and mortar and sweeping windows, varilevel porches and patios, the lower levels built into the hillside and exploiting the natural topography to the maximum. Shown a photo of the Frenchi estate, one would think the setting to be one of isolated seclusion; in reality it was the scene of an exclusive neighborhood of millionaires. Frenchi had merely gotten there first and carved out the large and commanding site; the others had followed.

One rumor had it that Frenchi had accumulated his fortune in the export-import business; another, that he had been a shipping magnate. The first story was closer to the truth—Frenchi's rise to riches had been chiefly through the international traffic in illegal drugs. He also had much reason to thank organized prostitution, bootlegging, gambling, and various other illegal American pastimes. In recent years, and especially in the impetus received during the Robert Kennedy Attorney-General days, Frenchi had been "legitimizing" his interests to every extent possible. He actually did own a small shipping line now, and his other latter-day interests included a string of loan companies and various small businesses, all lumped into the loose coagulation which was "Frenchi Enterprises."

First, last, and always, however, Sergio Frenchi was a "Family" man—the Mafia family. It was not a family one could disinherit or disclaim, even had he been so inclined. The family vows were a lifetime oath of primary allegiance, with all other considerations—including even marriage and fatherhood—falling into subservience to the higher obligation to the Mafia—God Himself and the church itself even stood in line behind the all-demanding sacred vows to the Mafia. Sergio Frenchi had been married to the same woman for 41 years, but it had been a barren marriage; there was no seed of Sergio Frenchi to immortalize this man. A warm and loving man, on his one side, Sergio filled this lack of his own loins with the products of other marriages close to him; he was "Uncle" Sergio to many, "Father" Sergio to a choice few —and Leopold Turrin was one of those latter. The Turrin children were as much at home in the sprawling Mediterranean villa as in their own residence; Angelina Turrin, orphaned at the age of ten, had actually come to think of Father Sergio as the grandfather of his children. Mother Frenchi had spent most of the past decade in traveling about the world; she was often present in the conversation of the Frenchi mansion but rarely seen in the flesh.

On this late morning of early September the Frenchi villa seemed much the same as always to Angelina Turrin, except that there were a few more cars in the drive than usual. The Turrin children leapt from the family convertible and raced excitedly up the stone steps to the sun deck in their usual display of animated greeting. Leo gave his wife's hand a comforting pat and left her standing beside the car; he followed a trail around to a rear stairway and disappeared from her view.

It was funny, she was thinking, how a person's world can change almost overnight. The big house she had loved so, for so many years, now seemed threatening and foreboding of evil. She wondered if she could go through the motions of warm cheer and happy association, just as though nothing at all had been changed in her life, just as though Father Sergio was still the warmly loving *nonno* of her earlier ignorance. She shivered, though the sun's rays were warm on her skin, and followed the children up the steps.

Her husband had come here to plot a man's death. He was sitting down in the midst of racketeers and murderers, while his children frolicked in the sunshine outside, to work out the grisly details for the entrapment and extinction of another human being. Angelina herself, of course, had come painfully close to snuffing out that very life, but for her it had been a wild panic of reaction to an impossible situation. She could still not remember actually pulling the trigger—thank God she had, of course, thank God for that panicky reaction. But to sit and *plot* . . . She shivered again and forced her legs to keep moving her up the steps. Perhaps reaction was a relative thing, she reasoned. Perhaps the reaction of these men was no different from hers—it was a matter of survival, and they were reacting in the only rational manner available to them. And perhaps some day she would forgive Leo for his underworld ties. And maybe —maybe she would end up like Mother Frenchi, moving aimlessly about the corners of the world to avoid the confrontation with reality in her own living room. *What is the profit for a man to gain the world, only to lose* . . . She abruptly snapped off the chain of thought, blinked back the tears, and went in search of her children.

They had learned from the earlier experience. The meeting was being conducted behind drawn blinds. A security force of twenty men had been moved onto the property, and an additional dozen quietly patrolled the neighborhood.

"So our little Angelina very nearly did the job a small army could not do, eh?" Sergio said, his voice heavy with sarcasm. "With a little toy of a pop-pop gun—eh?" He laughed, and turned chiding eyes onto an uncomfortable Leo Turrin. "You married well, Leopold. You take good care of that little lady. She will make a man of you yet."

"I'm just glad she was there," Turrin muttered. "She saved my life. You ever feel the muzzle of cold steel against the back of your head? Hell, I'm just glad she was there."

"And you have no apologies," Sergio observed quietly.

"Hell, I told you how it happened. All of a sudden, blam, there he was. And I didn't call those cops. Hell, they were all around the place. I'm just surprised that Bolan got away from them. I'm telling you, they were all around the place. It was like a police ball, and they were holding it at *my* place."

"I said you have no apologies. You know what I think?" The old eyes shifted about to take in the expectant stares lifted to him. "I think this guy is working with the cops. Not the locals—no, not the locals. He is an import—I think he's federal. Maybe he's CIA or something, with a license to kill. You know?"

A small man at the far end of the table shifted nervously, cleared his throat, and said: "Doesn't sound logical, Sergio. I'm sure I would have gotten wind of anything like that. Believe me, the department is going all out to get this guy."

Sergio fixed the speaker with a stern gaze. "And you would know about all these things, hah? You were too important to be bypassed on a hush-hush federal game, hah?"

The other man nodded his head. "Yes, I am. You know I am. I've never steered you wrong before, have I?"

"They've tried *every way* to bust us!" Sergio cried, suddenly emotional and pounding the table with his fist to emphasize the words. "Now why wouldn't they try *this?* Eh?"

"It's just alien to the American way," the small man replied, his voice taking on a clearly placating tone. "They simply do not operate that way, not against American citizens at any rate."

"But look at who has been killed!" Sergio retorted. "Have any of *us* been shot? Huh? Or even shot *at?* No. *No!* A man who can shoot a glass almost out of my hands can shoot *Sergio* if he wants to! Huh? Can't he?"

"What do you think he's up to, Sergio?" Plasky asked.

"Psychological warfare!" the old man snapped. "This is what he is up to. And maybe . . ." The eyes took on a dreamy look. "Maybe, *bambini,* maybe this Bolan is more than one man."

A long silence followed the declaration, all eyes on Sergio. He took his seat, fiddled with a cocktail napkin, then continued the line of thought. "Look at it," he said softly. "Just look. Five people are shot down in the street outside our Triangle office. Nobody sees the assassin, eh? This soldier shows up at Nathan's place, he is seen for the first time, and he cons our college-man Walter into a place in the organization. As soon as he has had time to learn a few faces and a few places of business, we get word through our *intelligence—*" He raised his eyes and scowled at the man at the end of the table. "—through our *intelligence* that this soldier is the assassin of our Triangle people, and that he is out to get us all. *So!* We get the contract out for this assassin, and he is there waiting for our contractors, eh? Again, he is not seen by anybody now living. He puts in an appearance at one of Leopold's places, but again he is seen only momentarily, and who is to say that the man who set the fire is the same man who fired senseless shots into an automobile, eh? Again, at Walter's home, a man who fits the general description of our soldier has a conversation with the kitchen woman—but who can say how many other men were on that property, eh?

"See what is a-building here, *bambini?* An *image.* An *image* of an invincible ghost who walks among us unseen and untouched, killing and destroying at will—an *image* of *fear,* eh?"

The men around the table, exactly twelve in number, were beginning to get excited. There were murmurings and creakings of chairs. Several cigars and a half-dozen cigarettes were lighted.

Sergio seemed to be enjoying his role immensely. He

was smiling now, expansively so. "You begin to see, eh? Our *intelligence* is not so *hot*, eh? The Mafia is getting soft, they say. Too much easy living, they say. The new generation of the family are mush-heads, they say. Let us shake their brains, they say. Let us push them as far as they will push, and see what mistakes they will make, eh? Let us play *games* with the Mafia, and maybe their panic will bring their house down. Eh?"

"I don't like this situation as much as the other one," Seymour commented sourly. "One lone guy, even a ghost, gives me a lot more comfort than a concentrated assault by the federal government, and with no regard for the rules of play."

"Comfort?" Sergio thundered. "You want *comfort*? Take your comfort, college man, and *sleep* with it! Sergio Frenchi wants a *dead Bolan!* Not a ghost, not an invincible destroyer, but a *dead body.*"

"But you just said . . ." Seymour began weakly, then lost steam altogether.

"I said you should get some bone in your back," the old man said sternly. "Forget all this whimpering and weeping about the Bolan *ghost*. *Make* him a ghost, a real one, and tell the feds to send us another. And we will make *him* a ghost, and tell them to send us another. Eh? Who is the *bold* and the *brave*, eh? Eh, Leopold? Is it our *women*?"

"We'll get the bastard," Turrin declared grimly, his eyes falling away from the old man's.

"Yes, yes we will. And this is *how* we will. Now, Nathan, first of all you will . . ."

And so began the council of September First. Angelina Turrin's foreboding of evil could well have been shared by Executioner Mack Bolan. And she had provided the lull that made it all possible. The Mafia had found a second wind, and it was to be an ill one for The Executioner.

BOOK THREE:

1—In With the New

Mack Bolan had, for more than 48 hours, been a guest in the apartment of Valentina Querente. He had learned that she was a teacher of history at the local high school, coincidentally the same school to which Bolan had been assigned as ROTC instructor—an assignment he would never fill. He had learned also that she was 26 years of age, single, given to swift changes of mood from the deeply sober to the richly humorous, that she appeared to be both virginal and worldly-wise, easily embarrassed by the most innocent of things while entirely at ease with some of the most sexually suggestive. They shared the same bed, with a rolled blanket separating them, Bolan practically naked in nothing but jockey shorts, Valentina well-bundled in a bulky gown. Her hands moved freely upon him in an assistance to his awkward attempts at dressing and undressing and he had observed her on several occasions in nothing more than panties and bra, yet their bodies had never touched, nor had their lips—not even their hands.

Bolan awoke to his third morning in the Querente bed with the lovely young woman seated beside him and peering into his face. "Hi," he said. Her eyes shifted away from his in obvious embarrassment.

"You always wake up and catch me staring at you," she complained.

"I really can't think of a nicer way to wake up," he told her. His hand found hers and enfolded it, for the first time.

"Don't, uh—you'd better not," she said breathlessly, feebly attempting a withdrawal from his grasp.

"Why not? It's a nice, soft little hand, entirely comforting to hold."

"It, uh, that's your sore arm."

"It isn't all that sore now. I could probably even hug you with it."

"Get serious, Mack," she said soberly. "Really—the reason I was sitting here like this—I mean—well, it's about time you left the nest, isn't it?"

"You kicking me out?" he asked.

She nodded her head. "Especially if you're feeling all that strong."

"All what strong?" he asked whimsically.

"All that strong to hug me with your sore arm."

"Lie down here and let's give it a test run," he suggested.

"I want to," she replied, her eyes unwavering. "That's why I think . . ."

"That I'd better be leaving?" he said.

"Uh-huh." She withdrew the hand from Bolan's and clasped both her hands nervously in her lap.

"Have you ever been in love, Valentina?" Bolan asked softly.

"Oh gosh, please don't start—"

"No fooling," he said, "and no line. Have you ever been in love?"

"Of course," she replied. "Two or three times."

"What does it feel like?"

There was a brief silence, then: "You *are* serious, aren't you?"

"I said I was."

"Well I just said that. I don't know how it feels to be in love. I mean, really in *love*. I've had crushes. I think I have one on you, now. I think."

He chose to ignore the not-so-surprising declaration. "I'm thirty years old," he said musingly.

"I know that."

"Years ago, a lot of years ago, I used to think that someday I'd fall in love with some girl."

"How many years ago?"

"I don't remember thinking much about it for a long time now. Long time. All of a sudden I'm thinking about it again. How come?" He was staring at her intently, as though perhaps expecting to find the answer to his question in that stare.

"Oh, Mack—please—don't . . ."

His arms went about her and he pulled her onto him; her face was suspended directly above his, eyes large and frightened. "Mack, please don't let's be in love," she whispered. "I don't want to be in love with a murderer."

His eyes froze and she saw the veils sliding across them. He released her and she flung herself away from the bed and lurched through the door. Bolan was muttering beneath his breath. He swung his feet to the floor and looked about for his clothing. He could hear Valentina sobbing, in another room. "Thanks," he muttered. "Thanks for reminding me." He went into the bathroom, found his clothes hanging just where they'd been that first morning, relocated them atop the vanity, turned on the water, and stepped into the shower. He removed the bandage from his shoulder, slid back the shower curtain, and inspected the wound in the mirror. He decided that soap and water would not hurt it any, closed the curtain, and took a leisurely bath. Then he dressed and went into the kitchen. Valentina had his breakfast waiting for him, but she was nowhere in evidence.

He ate mechanically, in sober contemplation, and he had finished a cigarette and was working on his third cup of coffee when he heard the front door open. Valentina appeared a moment later, slightly breathless, very lovely in shorts and bare-midriff blouse.

"I moved your car again," she told him, sinking into a chair opposite his and regarding him with misty eyes.

"Thanks," he said softly. "I'd like to give you a citation

for service above and beyond, or something. I guess instead I'll just give you ten grand."

"Ten what?"

"There's a lot of money in the trunk of that car. I'm going to give you ten thousand of it."

"I don't want any money," she said, eyes clouding. "Anyway, where'd you get it?"

"The money?" He smiled and took time to light another cigarette. "Well, besides being a murderer, I'm also a thief, but that's something that did not get reported. They couldn't afford to report it. I stole a quarter of a million of the Mafia's *secret bucks.*"

"My gosh!" she cried. "All that money is out there in that car?"

He nodded. "And I intend to keep it. There's no telling how long this war will last, and it takes money to wage war. So—I'll fight 'em with their own money. See? I not only kill, but I also steal, cheat, and lie."

"I—I don't really think of you as a murderer, Mack," she said contritely. "I—don't know why I said that."

"No, you're right," he told her. "School starts tomorrow and you'll be going back to the classroom, I'll be going back to the battlefield. That's the way it has to be, and there simply is no room for anything in between." He looked at her and grinned. "I'm sorry I lost my head."

"I—I really don't think of you as a murderer," she repeated, avoiding his gaze. "—and I'm uh, not going to kick you out of the nest, either. You can stay as long as you'd like, but you'll have to sleep on the couch from now on. Unless . . ."

Bolan's eyebrows raised. "Unless what?"

"Unless nothing," she mumbled. "I guess I'm not kicking you out of my bed either." She underwent one of those lightning changes of moods, smiling impishly, eyes sparkling. "Twenty-six, never kissed, and never a man in my bed—until you. Now you don't think I'll let you out all *that* easy, do you?"

"I just might slap you silly," he growled, dropping his eyes to the coffee cup.

"All righty, I'll even let you slap me silly." A tear oozed out of each eye and slid silently down the smooth cheeks. Their eyes met and Bolan knew a wrenching of the heart he had never before experienced.

"God, Val!" he groaned. They left their chairs simultaneously, meeting at the end of the table and falling fiercely into each other's arms. Bolan ignored the tiny twinge at his shoulder and clasped her in tight enfoldment. Her face tilted to his, lips moistly parted, and her mouth grafted to his with consuming urgency, the petite body melting into him in total surrender. His hands moved automatically to the vibrant flesh between shorts and blouse and she twisted against him with a racking sob. She dragged her lips away from his and moaned, "I can't help it, Mack, I just can't help it."

Without a word he lifted her off her feet and carried her into the bedroom, she clinging to him and moaning breathless little sounds into his ear. He stood her up on the bed and undressed her, placing a moist kiss upon each of her hips and upon the delicately folded belly button. Her fingers curled into his hair and she shuddered, then dropped to her knees, arms about his neck, mouth hungrily seeking his as she wriggled against him. She pulled away abruptly, weakly gasping, "Oh, oh, oh." His lips nuzzled into her throat and followed the delicate contours onto firm little breasts, the nipples of which were stiffly extended and vibrantly responsive.

"Let me—help—you," she panted, her fingers twisting ineffectually at his clothing.

Bolan gently pushed her hands away and disrobed himself. She fell back onto the pillow and lay very still, gazing up at him with glistening eyes. "I love you, Mack Bolan," she whispered.

"Thank you," he said softly, settling beside her.

"You're quite welcome," she gasped.

"You, uh, have to put your legs, Val—uh, like this."

"Oh, oh Mack!"

"God, you're sweet. You're so damn sweet, Val."

"I—love you—Mack."

"I love you too, Val."

"Oh, Mack—oh—*Mack!*"

"God, Val, God!"

"Oh Mack! Oh Mack! *Oh Mack!*"

And so ended the lull for Executioner Bolan.

2—The Whole Truth

She was curled loosely into his arms, lying half atop him in utter relaxation. There had been a long period of silence when she stirred slightly and rocked her face out of the hollow of his shoulder. "I don't think I . . ." she began, then lapsed back into silence.

"Huh?"

"I was going to say I didn't want today to ever end. But it must, of course. Regardless of what happens next, though, I'm glad and—and thankful for—for this."

He twisted around and kissed her, then said, "I'm sorry it has to be this way, Valentina. You deserve better —a lot better."

"I guess I couldn't stand it much better," she replied, smiling shyly.

"You should at least be able to love a man you approve of," he told her.

"Resist not evil," she whispered.

"Huh?"

"Get out of it!" she said urgently, twisting fully atop him and peering into his face. "Go away and forget about these people. There must be any number of safe places for you somewhere in the world. I'd go with you, Mack. I'd go anywhere you asked me to go."

"Now, wait a minute," he said feebly.

"It isn't right to kill, Mack," she persisted. "Even if you defeat them, if you exterminate them completely, you're the one who will end up the big loser. Violence is not the answer to evil."

Bolan returned her solemn stare. "You think we, uh, should live in a world of brotherly love—and turn the other cheek and that kind of stuff, eh?" he asked quietly.

His fingers were tracing the line of her spine. She

shivered and wriggled against him. "Don't do that," she breathed. "I'm trying to talk seriously."

"What could a fragile flower like you know about violence, and of the evil men do to one another?" he asked, smiling faintly.

"Evil is not received, Mack. Evil can only be given, and it can finally hurt only the giver."

"That's an interesting theory," Bolan replied. "Would you say that the Jews received no evil from Hitler?"

"Hitler was the ultimate receiver of all the evil he created."

"Yeah, but what if the whole world had just gone on turning the other cheek to Adolf? He would have just sliced that one open, too, and where would the world be now?"

"What has become of the world now?" Valentina asked sorrowfully. "We answered evil with evil. And in our end result, we have inherited evil."

He slapped her gently on the bottom. "Where'd you get such screwy ideas?" he asked her. "Look—there are two forces, two basic forces, loose in this world. Good and evil. Hell, I'm no crusader, Val, but I believe that good is more than just a lazy state of do-nothingness. Good has to be more energetic and more—more moving than the opposing force if it—if it's going to overcome."

They were silent for a long moment. Valentina lowered her face to his and nibbled his lower lip, dodged back with a tiny gasp and scrunched away from his questing hands. "How many people," she asked thoughtfully, "do you think set out to deliberately do evil? Even your own example, Adolf Hitler—don't you suppose he was acting in a movement toward what he regarded as ultimate good?"

"Sure," Bolan said agreeably. "But other people had other ideas about what was good, for them, and what was not—so they opposed him. Goodness, Val, is a very personal and individual thing. The way I see it. I'm an instinctive creature, see. Now take this Vietnam war. A lot of people think it is an evil war. Well—of course it is. But hell, we didn't start that evil, see, our side has simply chosen to oppose it, to oppose the evil. I personally go along with that idea, therefore I feel that I am on the side of good when I'm over there fighting that war. I would feel very evil myself if I hung back and didn't throw myself in there with the good guys. See? With me, it's a personal and instinctive thing. And I'm in the same sort of situation here, with this private little war I'm in now. I didn't start this mess, see. The Mafia has been having their own way in this country for a hell of a lot of years. Well, I finally saw the evil of the Mafia. I saw what they were doing and I felt the need to oppose them. It's as simple as that. You can take all the damn philosophies and beauty religions and peace movements and put them in a pile and they still won't mean as much as my individual, instinctive reaction to the Mafia. These people are a dripping, oozing, mass of evil draped about the throat of this country. I'm going to pry them loose if I can. Even if, in the end, the devil picks up all the marbles."

"It must be nice to have such a simple and uncomplicated view of the world," Valentina commented.

"Aw, come off it, Val," Bolan said half-irritably. "People like to play philosophic games with themselves, and they get all tangled up in the loose ends. Look at all these mixed up nuts parading around this country squalling about our 'immoral' war. If they feel all that strongly about it, why don't they go over and join the other side and fight for their idea of good."

"You are totally committed to the idea of violence and bloodshed, aren't you," she observed solemnly.

"No, I'm not. I'm committed to action. As long as I'm sitting around just yapping about good and evil, then I'm merely debating the question. And while I'm debating, evil might get the upper hand. No, Val. If I thought

I could march through the underworld tooting on a pipe and have all the hoods and goons and rats follow me to jail, then that's the way I'd go about it. What the hell are we arguing about? I didn't start this mess. The Mafia started it by just being. Being what they are. The mere fact that they are what they are has challenged me. I've answered the challenge, that's all. And yes, in this instance, I am committed to violence and bloodshed."

"War without end," she sighed.

"Yes, war without end." He ran both hands along her back and onto the tight little buttocks. "There's no way to break off now, anyway. It's Bolan against the world now, Val. Surely you recognize that. I'll never be a free man again, not ever again. The law of the land feels bound to call me into an accounting for my 'crimes.' You see, my private little war is an immoral war, also. So, the law is after me. The Army is after me, and pretty soon I'll be declared a deserter. The underworld is after me. And now, now my dear little idealist, *you* are after me. I guess it's Bolan against the world."

"Is your recruiting station open?" she whispered.

"Huh?"

Her arms snaked around his neck and she squeezed against him with an almost desperate intensity. Her face, on his, was moist with tears. "I'd like to join Bolan's side," she whispered. "Are enlistments open?"

He rolled to his side, carrying her with him. She groaned deliciously and looped both legs high about him. "You're joining a sure loser," he warned her.

"I don't know about that," she replied, smiling through tears. "You seem rather capable to me."

"Your confidence is overwhelming," he said, joining her smoothly and thoroughly.

Her eyes were wide pools of essential truth. "So's yours," she sighed happily.

3—Forecast: Warmer Tonight and Tomorrow

It had been dark for several hours. The Executioner was in battle dress and ready for combat. His woman was clinging to him in a farewell kiss. One of her hands dropped onto the holstered .45 at his waist and bounced hastily away. "Be careful," she whispered. "Come back to me."

"I'll be back," he assured her. "Maybe not tonight. Maybe not even tomorrow. But I'll be back."

"It's been a glorious honeymoon," she sighed.

"But too short," he said, grinning.

She nodded, smiling bravely. "Entirely too short." She ran a finger lightly along his left temple. "Think your hair will grow back there?"

"I'm just glad I didn't lose an ear," he told her.

Her hand fell to his left shoulder. "Sure your shoulder is all right?"

"I'm just glad it wasn't the right one," he replied.

"You're just glad about everything aren't you?" she said, wrinkling her nose.

"If you'd ever had the butt of a heavy rifle bucking into your shoulder you'd be glad, too," he told her, his face soberly reflective.

"Mack Bolan, I believe you are bloodthirsty. You're just itching to get back into the fray, aren't you."

"To tell the truth, no," he replied, grinning again. "It's always just a little harder after a wounding."

She pounced quickly. "Then why don't you just—"

He'd draped a hand across her lips. "Don't start that again," he commanded gently. "Look—if something goes wrong and I get pinned down somewhere, I'll at least try to get a call to you. But don't get shook if you don't hear from me. Silence, in warfare, is often no more than the better part of valor. Understand? Stay cool."

"I'll stay cool," she assured him.

He turned out the lights, went to the door and opened it, looked back at her briefly, then he was gone. She ran to the door to gaze after him, but already he was swallowed into the night. She closed the door, shoulders slumping wearily, and cried quietly for several minutes. Such a dramatic change her life had undergone. She snapped the lights back on and gazed about the small apartment, looking for evidence of the change. There was no evidence, she decided. All the evidence had walked out the door moments earlier. She squared her shoulders, went to the television set and turned it on, and settled into the long vigil. He *would* be back. He would. He would.

Bolan stopped at the first secluded public telephone on his route and made a call to Lieutenant Al Weatherbee. "It's funny," he told him, "every time I call I find you there, no matter when. What are you—married to that job?"

"Bolan?" Weatherbee asked, his voice rising on the last syllable.

"Yeah. I just got back from my holiday on the Riviera, wondered if you'd missed me."

"Aw shit," Weatherbee fumed, "—just when I was beginning to hope I'd gotten you outta my hair for good. Bolan, why aren't you in Mexico?"

"No action down there," Bolan replied. "I've been watching the TV, by the way, so I've heard all the rumors. I haven't been in Mexico, or in South America, I've been right here all along. What have our little friends been up to?"

"This's no private detective agency, Bolan," Weatherbee groused. "You've got a hell of a nerve calling here, anyway. You're wanted on eleven counts of murder, among other things."

"Yeah, I feel terrible about all that," Bolan replied, chuckling. "But don't worry about it, Lieutenant, I believe the count will be upped somewhat before the next dawn."

"Bolan, for God's sake, let it rest where it is. Listen, there's a lot of unofficial and public sympathy for you now. If you've been watching the TV you must realize that. Come on in now. Or tell me where you are and I'll pick you up personally. Two of the best lawyers in the country have already expressed an interest in your case, and I can almost—"

"Save it, Lieutenant," Bolan clipped in. "Nothing is resting, and especially the Mafia—right?"

"You damn better know *right,*" the policeman clipped back. "You can bet they've been making full use of this breather you've given them. They're ready and waiting for you now."

"Yeah, I figured that. That's why I called. Wondering if you had any useful information to pass along."

The policeman's heavy breathing filled the wire for several seconds, then he said: "Why should I tell you a damn thing!"

"Because you know I'm on your side, that's why."

"The hell you are!"

"Sure I am, and I don't have all your restrictions. I've shaken these people like they've never been shook be-before, and you know it. Now just who's side are you on, Weatherbee?"

"It isn't a matter of *sides!*" the cop roared. "It's a—a . . ."

"Yeah, a technicality. Okay, play the technicalities if you want to. But I'd sure like to know what they've been up to."

"They think you're working for us," Weatherbee said, nearly choking.

"There, you see? *They* don't deal in technicalities, do they."

"They've got commando teams of their own now. The first time you open up on them again, you're going to get hit with everything short of the atom bomb."

"Is that right?"

"That's right. It's hopeless, Bolan. You had them reeling once, but they've consolidated now. The first offensive action that gives away your position will be your last one. You're just lousing things up, like all amateurs are bound to do. You've come very close to destroying a five-year undercover operation we've had going against this bunch."

There was a momentary silence, then: "You've got an undercover operation going?"

"Of course we have. Where do you think we've been getting all this information I'm passing to you?"

"Five years, eh? How many more years had you planned on staying undercover?"

"Forever if necessary. We're interested in nailing these people good, Bolan. We've just been waiting for the proper moment."

"For *five years?* You have any idea how much hell these people have brought to earth during those five years?"

The policeman's voice was growing heavy with exasperation. "We know what we're doing."

"I know what I'm doing, too," Bolan told him. "And I'm not taking any five damn years to do it, either. Keep your cops away from me, Weatherbee. I'm hitting them again tonight."

"We'll stop you if we can!"

"You can't. All you can do is provide aid and comfort to the mutual enemy. Keep your cops away. I'm hitting tonight."

Bolan broke the connection, returned to his car, and sat quietly pondering the conversation with Weatherbee.

The cop had been right, of course. The campaign had moved into a dimension which seemed impossibly weighted against him.

Mack Bolan was a military realist. In the traditional strategems of warfare, a superior force spelled victory over an inferior one; superiority, however, had never been an item of mere numbers. An elite platoon could easily take on a green company; one lone tank could devastate a field of foot soldiers. In Vietnam, firepower and mobility had become the catchwords of military superiority. Bolan had learned well the lessons of military survival. He was not an idle dreamer, and he had never had much respect for banzai warfare. He needed an equalizer. His strategy had thus far paid off; it had accomplished his aims. He had forced the enemy to reveal its position. He had smoked them out of their bunkers of social respectability and made it necessary that they regroup and reform and expose themselves even further. But—as Bolan well knew—he had accomplished this initial objective at the cost of a vital military necessity: he had lost the edge of superiority which had carried his campaign this far.

Weatherbee's assessment of the situation had been an accurate one. The *Mafiosi* would be alert and ready this time, and undoubtedly with some tricky defensive tactics of their own. Bolan's next offensive action would undoubtedly be little more than a hopeless banzai attack—unless ... A lone rifleman could not hope to successfully take on an entire enemy company—unless ... Bolan grinned suddenly, started the engine, and moved out into no-man's land. Superiority, he reminded himself, was not an item of mere numbers.

He drove directly to the industrial district on the south edge of the city, then turned into a warehouse complex, vague memories stirring and fighting to the surface of mind. Several years earlier, Bolan had spent several weeks on special assignment at one of these warehouses. If he could just find the right one . . .

He located it easily, a low-slung, corrugated steel structure with a peculiarly flat roof, the now-weathered sign—SURPLUS EXPORTS, INC.—and the smaller decal: MDI—which, Bolan recalled, were the initials for Munitions Distributors International.

As a skilled armorer, Bolan had been assigned temporarily to assist in the cataloguing and storing of a large shipment of surplused weapons and ammunition which had been sold to the firm by the Government. Many of the items Bolan had handled during that assignment had never been used, though there had also been genuine surpluses dating back to the Second World War. The stuff could not be sold to private citizens in the U.S., but the export business in these materials had been quite active at the time of Bolan's involvement. He was hoping that the Vietnam escalations had not shut off the source of supply. In the back of his mind had long lurked the suspicion that many of the so-called war surpluses were not, in fact, surpluses at all, but Government goofs of overproduction and oversupply. Still—the shipment which Bolan had been assigned to catalogue had been bona fide surpluses of obsolete weaponry. He would be quite content to get his hands on three or four of these "obsolete" weapons.

Bolan left the car in the shadows of the freight dock and circled the building on foot in a cautious reconnoiter, simultaneously searching his memory for the security details. Then he returned to the car, buckled on a tool kit, and fished a packet of U.S. currency from the spare-tire well. He had decided upon his mode of entry.

Ten minutes later he was scooting along the interior of a ventilation shaft; soon thereafter he had located the "special weapons" area and was shopping grimly and methodically for the advantages of military superiority, jotting down the nomenclature and estimated dollar value of each item on a sheet of paper.

He double-checked the completed list, totalled the dollar value, added a ten percent "error factor," and left the list and the money in a conspicuous place. A thief, Bolan reminded himself, he was not. Besides, he ruminated darkly, it was especially fitting that the enemy's money was paying for this purchase.

He disabled the alarm system, boldly rolled open the door to the freight dock, loaded the hardware into his car, then went back inside and resecured the building, exiting the same way he had gained entry. As he was driving away, Bolan spotted the patrol car of the private security guard assigned to the protection of the complex, cruising slowly in the opposite direction. Bolan grinned and gunned up onto the highway. Step One, *equalization,* had gone off without a hitch. A "smoke-out" mission was next on tap.

4—Prelude

Bolan left the car at the rear entrance to the apartment building and went up the service elevator to the fifth floor, padded softly down the hall to a door marked "511" and leaned on the doorbell. Forty seconds or so later he heard sounds within the apartment and a male voice called, "Okay, okay, just a minute."

He let up on the button and braced his good shoulder against the door. As soon as it cracked he shoved on in, nearly upsetting the man on the other side. "Wha—what . . . ?" the man stuttered.

"You know me," Bolan snapped. "Get dressed. We're going out."

The man turned and ran toward the rear of the apartment, but Bolan was right with him. He grabbed an arm and swung the fleeing man around, driving a balled fist into his midsection. The man's breath left him in a loud grunt and he sank limply onto a small table. Bolan steadied him there until he was breathing normally again, then shoved him roughly toward the bedroom.

Several minutes later they left the apartment together, went down the back way, and got into Bolan's car. Not a word had passed between them since the original confrontation at the door to the apartment. Now the man gawked at the canvas-covered bulk in the back seat of the car and said: "What's that back there?"

"It could be dead bodies," Bolan replied quietly. "You could end up back there if you get stupid."

The man jerked around and faced stonily forward. A short drive later they were at the offices of Escorts Unlimited. The man opened the door and no outward sign of reluctance, and Bolan followed him inside.

"What are we doing here?" the man asked.

"Not *we—you,*" Bolan replied. "You're going to give me a print-out on the entire prostitution operation. I want it all—call girls, house girls, streetwalkers, the whole thing. And I want it damn quick."

"Yes, sir," the programmer quickly agreed.

"Punch the wrong button and it'll be your death program. Make sure you understand that. If I get what I want, that's all I want. But if you screw me up, I'll screw you up. Understand?"

"Yes, sir, I understand."

Twenty minutes later they were going back out the door. Bolan was carrying a large manila envelope. "This is to be just between you and me," Bolan told him. "If I find out you've been talking about it, I'll figure you decided to try to screw me up. Understand?"

"Yes, sir, I understand," the programmer replied meekly.

Bolan left him on the sidewalk, got into his car, and drove off. He really did not give a damn if the programmer talked or not. But after he was finished with the lists, he'd mail them to Lieutenant Weatherbee. Perhaps they could be of some police value if the secret was maintained until that time. He glanced at his watch. It was just past one o'clock. The night had hardly begun. His face twisted into a wry smile. It was going to be a hellish night.

Bolan walked down a darkened hallway, paused in front of a door and held his ear to it for a moment, then leaned back against the opposite wall and opened the door abruptly with a swift kick. The scene that greeted him through the open doorway could have been a pornographic snapshot. An attractive young woman was holding a nude hands-and-knees stance atop a disarrayed bed, positioned crosswise with her feet and the calves of her legs protruding out over the side. A nude man stood between the protruding calves, thrusting vigorously from the waist, his hands tightly gripping the girl's hips. Both man and woman were staring at Bolan with dumbfounded amazement, though the man's physical activities seemed hardly disturbed by the intrusion. There was a strangely unreal quality to the scene, grotesquely silent and dreamlike. Bolan stepped into the room and delivered a smashing backhand blow to the man's face; he released the girl's hips and stumbled back across the room. Bolan felt bad about that, but he reminded himself that there was no morality in a holy war. The same hand that had disconnected the man swung back in a vicious open-hand slap to the girl's poised buttocks. She yowled and fell forward across the bed, then flipped to her side and lay there screaming obscenities. Her erstwhile companion scooped up a ball of clothes and scampered out of the room. A door was flung open down the hall and a youth of about 25 ran into the room shortly thereafter, a wicked-looking knife in one hand. Bolan took the knife away from him and tossed him across the room and into the wall. The girl stopped screaming and stared stupidly at the crumpled figure of the youth. Bolan turned to her and showed her his teeth. "Any more girls at work here?" he snarled.

She shook her head emphatically. "D-downstairs, in the bar," she gasped.

"We'll see," Bolan said. He strode from the room and began opening other doors along the hallway. There were six in all, and he scored again on the last one. Two naked women were on the bed, rolled together in a tight knot of arms and legs. Bolan could not see the head of either. "Didn't anybody hear the ruckus?" he asked loudly, then thrust a hand into the tangle and pulled them onto the floor. The ecstatic expression on the face of a woman of about 45 had quickly converted to one of baffled torment. "What is—get out of here!" she cried.

"Which of you is the working girl?" Bolan asked, grinning.

A well-proportioned younger woman slowly rose to her feet, giving Bolan a frightened once-over. "Where's your whip?" she asked sullenly.

"Right here," Bolan replied calmly. He thwacked her across the bottom with an open hand and shoved her back onto the bed, snared the older woman's clothing from a nearby chair and pushed her out the door, draping the clothing about her neck. "You'd better leave damn quick," he said, curling his lips menacingly. "I'm about to shoot up the joint."

The woman had started crying. She hurried down the hall and shot out the door, still naked. Bolan grinned and stepped back inside the invaded room. The girl was cringing on the bed, twisted bedcovers hastily pulled across her middle. "Tell Leo I don't like his Main Street joints," Bolan said. He tossed a marksman's medal onto the bed. "Tell 'im!"

He left then and went silently down the back stairs to the alley, got into his car, and departed. Ten minutes later he pulled up at the back of a townhouse complex, consulted one of the lists from the manila envelope, smiled, and went to the back door. He returned to the car a moment later, took a crowbar from the back floor, and went back to the rear door of the building. A well-placed lever-action and a dull snap later the door was open, and The Executioner was inside. He was in a small service hall; he could see the kitchen through a glass porthole in a door to his right, another door was set into the far wall. Things were swinging on the other side of that door; a hi-fi going full blast and other sounds of merriment told the story quite vividly. He went in through the kitchen door, unholstered the .45, and immediately bumped into a nude girl who was leaning drunkenly across a tiled drainboard, vainly attempting to free ice cubes from a frosted tray.

"You're going to freeze a tit," he warned her, and brushed on past.

"Fat chance," she mumbled, hardly noticing him otherwise.

It was a large living room, richly appointed with oriental rugs and tapestries and further decorated with wall-to-wall living flesh. The lights were low and nobody seemed to be moving about, but the conversation from the floor level was animated and unrestrained. Nobody seemed to be aware of Bolan's presence. He went back through the kitchen, paused long enough to flip the ice cubes onto the drainboard for the nude girl, allowed her to kiss him in reward, then stepped onto the service porch and inspected the plumbing fittings of the laundry trays. He'd noticed the garden hose outside, on his way in; he went outside and brought it back in with him, screwed one end onto the fitting at the laundry plumbing, looped the other end over in a closing pinch, and turned on the cold water full force, then went back through the kitchen and to the living room, patting the ice-seeker's derrière on the way through, dragging the hose with him. He found the wall with the light switch and brought the overhead lights into the action. A murmuring arose and someone said loudly, "What's with the lights?" Bolan guessed that perhaps thirty people were present, all nude, and all bound together somehow in a confusing tangle of limbs and torsos. A girl in the center was beginning to shriek in a calmly controlled fashion; Bolan's roving eye found her and noted that she was the recipient of multiple attentions, any one of which would have no doubt proved sufficient to produce the muffled little shrieks.

Another person shouted an obscenity concerning the bright lights. Bolan shook his head regretfully, and bawled: "Look alive, everybody. The Executioner's here!" Even then the reaction was limited to two or three startled raisings of heads. He thumbed off the safety of the .45 and crashed a single shot into the hi-fi set. It stopped its noise instantly, even before the thundering roar of the heavy gun had ceased reverberating through the tightly packed room. Everybody was staring at him now in shocked attention. He released the kink at the end of the garden hose and sprayed the cold water liberally over all, hating himself for the bastard he was all the while.

There was a new tenor to the shrieks and mouthings now. Men were cursing and floundering about while women screeched hysterically. Bolan flung the hose into the room, stepped back into the kitchen, grabbed the nude girl and kissed her again, balanced a marksman's medal on the slope of a high breast, and departed.

There was to be one more prelude stop. He selected it carefully and headed the car toward the suburbs. It was just past two-thirty in the morning when he parked in the shrubbery a hundred yards or so down from the secluded pleasure palace on the eastern rim of the city. He rummaged in the back seat of the car and came up with three canisters about the size of a large can of beans. He stuffed them into a pouch at his waist and set off at a cross-country angle toward the house. Lights shone from every window, though dim and muffled by concealing draperies. Judging from the number of automobiles in the parking area, they were having a good night. As he drew closer he could hear music, and every now and then a feminine laugh. He walked upright across the grounds, pausing every ten or twelve yards to stand still and listen. During one of those stops he heard male voices nearby; one man was laughing restrainedly. He moved toward the voices and located the source quickly. Two men stood with their backs to him, about fifty feet from the side of the large house; each of them held a sawed-off shotgun cradled loosely in the crook of an elbow; each seemed entirely relaxed. One was large and beefy; the other of medium height and weight, and the smaller one was speaking.

"Those guys are out of their minds," he said. "I

wouldn't give no two hundred and fifty bucks for no party."

"Augh, two-fifty to these types is no more than two bits to guys like us," the other man replied. "I'd give two bits any time for an orgy like that."

"I thought Leo was comin' by," the other side, shifting the shotgun about and digging into a pocket. He produced a cigarette and struck a kitchen match on the stock of the gun. "I ain't seen 'im, have you?"

The large man chuckled. "Naw, he won't be around tonight. Bet on that. Blacksuit's got 'em all walking around on eggs."

"I'd like to shove this fuckin' shotgun up Leo's ass. You know these things get *heavy* after a while."

"Lay it down then," said a soft voice behind them. "But do it carefully and very, very quietly. Your first sound will be your last."

The men exchanged glances. The smaller one thrust his shotgun straight out in front of him, at arm's length, then slowly bent to the ground with it and carefully set it down. The large man wanted to discuss the issue. "Says who?" he wanted to know, but staring rigidly forward.

"You were just discussing me," Bolan told him. "I wear a black skinsuit."

"How do I—"

His words were abruptly halted by the shock of a heavy .45 automatic moving forcefully against his temple. He crumpled and a black-clad arm reached out of the shadows and caught the shotgun, broke it at the breech, and tossed it to the ground. The sharp tip of a pointed blade touched lightly upon the smaller man's throat. "I have no bitch with you, buddy," the soft voice announced. "You just give me some useful information and you might live a while."

The man's lips moved soundlessly. He cleared his throat and tried again. "Anything you say," he croaked.

"How many guards?"

"Two more, just two more."

"Shotguns?"

"Yes. We weren't supposed to bunch up like this." He obviously wanted to keep talking. "I'm supposed to be at the front, Charlie had this side. Charlie's the guy you just conked. Matt's around at the back. Andy's got the other side. There's two guys inside, one upstairs in the hall, the other down at the front door. No shotguns, just shoulder holsters."

"Seems like a rather heavy guard for a whore house," the voice purred.

"Just since you started raisin' hell," the man replied, his voice taking on an ingratiating quality. "You got 'em shook up good, they even raised our pay."

"And a bonus to the one who gets me?"

"You ain't shittin', a bonus. A hundred grand worth of bonus."

"Don't you want to try for the bonus?"

"Me?" The tight throat was cleared again. "Who, me? Hell, no. I got nothin' against you, Blacksuit. Say, uh, the knife's about to bust through. It feels like it's gonna go through just any second now."

"Then be very still. Now, tell me . . ."

"Harry."

"Eh?"

"My name's Harry."

"Tell me, Harry, what's on the other side of that big window down here on the side?"

"Oh, that's uh, a sort of bar, you know. They can push back the walls in the middle there and it makes into a big clubroom. They got the walls back now and they're having a shindig in there right now. Yeah, right now."

"What sort of shindig, Harry?"

"You know, a sex party. An orgy."

"What's upstairs?"

"Bedrooms, just bedrooms. Oh, and a long hall and a

sittin' room. The upstairs guard station is just outside the sittin' room, in th' hall."

"What's on the other side of this party room, downstairs here?"

"Oh, well, I told you, they push the walls back, and it's all just one big room, clear across."

"How many people would you say are in there right now, Harry?"

"Oh, well, I can tell you exactly. I got the front detail, see. I checked thirty-two guys through. There's thirty-two in there, exactly."

"No girls?"

"Oh, well, yeah, there's girls. There's the twenty-five regulars and about, uh, oh I'd say about, uh fifteen or so specials."

"Specials for what?"

"Well, for the party. They move 'em around for these parties, see. Specialists."

"Specialists in what?"

"Different kinds of stunts, you know. Sex stunts."

"I see. Thank you, Harry. You've been very helpful. If I find out you've misled me, I'll come back and skin you."

"I ain't misled you."

"We will see," said The Executioner. He removed the pointed blade and immediately applied the .45 just behind the ear. The talkative informant fell over sideways without a sound. Bolan picked up his shotgun, checked it over for load and readiness, and carried it with him to the large window at the unguarded side of the house. He removed one of the canisters from his waist pouch and dropped it to the ground, then swung the shotgun against the window, dancing back to avoid flying fragments. The huge window went with a roaring crash; Bolan waited but a split second to clear any falling slivers, then thrust the muzzle of the shotgun against the exposed drapery, angling high toward the ceiling, and pulled both triggers. The double roar must have sounded like doomsday to those inside. A watermelon-sized hole appeared in the heavy drapery material. Bolan picked up the canister, flipped a lever at its top, and tossed it through the hole in the drapery. Heavy black smoke drifted back through the hole and billowed up between the drapery and the window frame. There were sounds of pandemonium within as Bolan hurried back to the fallen guards. He grabbed up the remaining shotgun and restored it to firing condition just as a man ran around the corner from the back side of the house. Bolan pushed the shotgun in the general direction of the running figure and pulled the trigger. The man was flung into the air like a rag doll, catching the full charge in the chest. Bolan swung to the sounds of thudding feet in the opposite direction and let go the other barrel. The target screamed and fell writhing to the ground, hands clutching at where his stomach had been. Bolan dropped the now-useless shotgun and got a grip on his .45 just as an upstairs window swung open and a man leaned out with a gun in his hand, foolishly exposing himself in full light.

The Executioner's .45 arced upwards and exploded once. The man's head snapped back and he disappeared from view. Bolan moved swiftly toward the front door, rounding the corner just as another man, gun at the ready, hurtled off the porch, firing wildly as he ran. Bolan dropped to one knee and his finger moved of its own accord, squeezing off two calculated shots at the running figure. The man stopped firing, stopped running, and began flopping about the ground. Bolan returned to the side of the house and tossed another smoke cannister into the open upstairs window, then dropped the last one on the ground and retreated behind the fast-forming cloud.

He regained his car, turned it around, and headed for

South Hills. The prelude skirmishes were at an end. The stage, he reflected grimly, should now be set for the big kill. He just hoped he hadn't overplayed the prelude music.

5—The Gathering

"Shit, I'm telling you the asshole is running wild again!" Plasky jabbered, pushing on into Sergio's bedroom. "Leo's on 'is way—"

"Wait a minute, wait a minute," the old man cried. "Calm down, will you." He shot a glance at his bodyguard and nodded his head calmly; the guard inclined his head slightly in an understanding and returned to his desk in the sitting room and picked up a house phone. Sergio sat stiffly upright at the edge of the bed, and said, "Now, Nathan, what is all this?"

"I said Bolan is at it again," Plasky replied, spacing his words in firm articulation, obviously smarting under the earlier shushing. "He hit three of Leo's places in less than an hour, and he killed four of the guards out at the Meadows. Leo is on his way out here now, and he's bringing Walt with him."

"Well, it's what we have been waiting for, isn't it?" Sergio replied, smiling calmly.

"Yeah, but hell, are you just going to sit there?"

"Would you like it better if I tried walking on the ceiling?"

"Aw hell, Sergio, we gotta man the ramparts. We gotta get the men—"

"Terry is seeing to those details at this moment," Sergio said, his eyes flicking past the open door and to the man at the desk. "Now simmer it down and get ahold of yourself. I'll tell you what. You go down to the council room and see that the stage is well set, eh?"

Plasky nodded his head jerkily. "Sure, sure Sergio, I'll make double-sure." He moved quickly out the door, past the guard desk, and along the hall to the large chamber on the second level.

The council table had been set, the chairs placed, and each one was occupied. Plasky smiled at the close attention to detail, readjusted an arm on one of the mannikins, and moved a wine bottle closer to the dummy hand. He walked about the table in a close inspection, hands clasped behind him like a proud maître d', then went to the window and inspected the positioning of the thin draperies that had been added during the reinstallation of the huge window glass. He stepped slowly about the room, checking the lighting, rechecking each little detail and wondering how it would look in shadow, through a sniperscope, and from perhaps a thousand yards distant. Then he punched a button on the hastily installed electronic device that would vary the lighting in a timed cycling and repositioning of light source, thus changing the projection of shadows onto the window-drapery. Plasky cackled inwardly as a shadowy arm was seen to move on the drapery, a head seemed to tip forward, a body appeared to lean across the table.

He had to see it again from outside. He hurried from the room and down the curving stairway and onto the patio, then sat on the wall and gazed up at the second-level window. Yeah, yeah, it was perfect, just perfect. The place looked alive, with a full council going on. Plasky grunted with satisfaction and paced about the flagstoned patio in hot anticipation of the little welcome The Family had in store for the sonuvabitch of the century.

Walt Seymour was about to burst with contained excitement. "How do we know he'll hit South Hills tonight?" he asked nervously, watching Turrin's face in the reflected glow of the instrument panel.

Turrin's teeth gleamed in a smile as he turned down the freeway ramp and began to climb into the exclusive neighborhood. "It's a thing the cops call *modus operandi*," he said. "Bolan isn't interested in stirring up our whorehouse operation, he just wants to stir *us* up. It worked for him once, he figures it'll work again. He sweeps in, see, and raises hell down in the grass roots to force us all to the council table. Then, he figures, he's got us all together and he can plunk us like rats in a water barrel, see. This is what we been waiting for, Walt."

"I wonder where the bastard's been all this time."

Turrin scowled. "Well—I hope he's just been licking his wounds. I'm positive Angie hit him the other night." The scowl deepened. "But from what I been hearing of his antics tonight—well—I dunno—he must o' not been hit too damn hard."

"He's probably onto us," Seymour said, his agitation visibly increasing. "He's probably been laying up there somewhere watching us all this time, probably with binoculars." He shivered. "Or through that damn sniper scope. How good are those scopes, Leo? You were in the service. They any damn good?"

"They're plenty damn good," Turrin replied. "Good enough to see a fly's pecker at fifteen hundred yards."

Seymour exploded into a mirthful fit. "A fly's *pecker*," he howled. Turrin grinned along with him, and he chuckled for a while, his tensions seeming to disintegrate in the penetrating good humor. "If that guy is fool enough to hit us again," he commented, following a long silence, "we'll nail his ass for good."

"Yes, I believe we will," Turrin agreed. But he was scowling again, and it was still with him when he turned into the hillside estate of Sergio Frenchi.

Bolan stopped at a public telephone in the darkened approaches to a closed service station, dropped in a dime, and dialed a rehearsed number. The receiver at the other end was lifted before the first ring could be completed and a trembly feminine voice said, "Yes?"

"This is the phantom of the bedroom," he announced pleasantly.

"Mack! Oh, Mack! Everything's okay?"

"Sure," he said. "But the night's still young. I just wanted to check in, let you know I'm still in the picture. I may be tied up the rest of the night? Uh—you been waiting up for me to call?"

Her reply came in a tumble of words. "Mack, I'll never go to bed again until it's with you. I tried, I really tried to, but that old bed just *shrieked* at me. No, I—I'm sitting up, I'm on the couch—oh Mack, don't let anything happen to you."

"It's not in the plan," he said, chuckling reassuringly. "I, uh, you know, Val, there's always a possibility of something going haywire, though. I forgot to tell you about the money. It's in a leather case, in the storage space above your hall closet. If anything—"

"I don't want the darned old money!" she cried.

"Just listen to me. If anything should go wrong, I want you to keep that money. Now, I mean it. Consider it as my estate. It's as much mine as anybody else's."

"Mack, you'd *better* come back here to me. You've just *got* to!"

"Hell, I'm sorry I mentioned it," he said uneasily. "Anyway—I've got this kid brother, see. You know about him. He could use some money, too, and—"

"Mack, I'm going to start screaming!"

"Don't do that," he said quickly. "Don't worry, it'll all come out okay. I just thought I should mention the money, just in case."

"I just want *you*." She was sobbing. "Call it off, Mack. Just come back. Come back right now."

"You're making it awfully tough on me, honey," he told her. "You know what I have to do."

She was regaining control. "All right," she said. "I'll be brave. Is this better?"

"Much better. Be a good girl now and go to bed. I want you nice and fresh when I get home."

"I'll try."

"I love you, Val."

"Oh God, Mack, I love you nutty!"

"It's great, isn't it." His voice was glowing.

"Yes, yes darling, it's great."

"Well—back to work. Stay cool, now."

"I promise. I'll stay cool. You do, too. And Mack . . ."

"Yeah?"

"I don't care who you have to kill, or how many. You come back here to me."

"I'll be back," he said, chuckling. He hung up, and his smile faded, and he stared glumly at the black box. It was odd, he reflected, how life came in bunches and gobs, and always at the wrong times. He had so much more to live for now than ever before, and he was facing the most perilous moment of his lifetime. He sighed, muttered, "I'll get back, Val,"—fingered a kiss onto the telephone mouthpiece, and The Executioner went off to join the gathering.

Lieutenant Al Weatherbee of the Metropolitan Police sleepily gathered his thermos jug and sandwiches and headed toward the police garage with his young sergeant, John Pappas. "Well, Johnny," he said tiredly, "if our intelligence is good, tonight will be the night."

"You say he knocked off three of their joints tonight?" Pappas asked, grinning.

"Yes, and don't look so happy about it. He's making us look like monkeys too, you know."

They stepped into the elevator and were silent in the descent to the garage. They stood quietly and waited as a half-dozen marked patrol cars gunned up the narrow ramp to the street, then went over to their squad car. Pappas slid behind the wheel and reached over to help

Weatherbee with his burden. "You planning on eating all this in one night?" he asked.

"Oh, between the two of us, I figure we can take care of it all right," the lieutenant replied. "And it could be a long, long night."

"Well, it's three o'clock already, and I just ate at two."

"It could still be a long time till breakfast." Weatherbee settled into the seat, nodded to his companion, and the car eased up the ramp.

"How many units they sending out?" Pappas wondered aloud.

"We'll have a dozen cars in the general area, eight of them assigned directly to us, the other four for backup as required. The sheriff is cooperating on this one, also. He's promised a minimum of ten men in the canyon, on the county side, and possibly some mounted units. I think we'll have him pretty well sewed up. If he shows, and I think he will, I don't see how he can possibly slip away from us this time. Unless . . ." Weatherbee scratched his cheek thoughtfully and showed his partner a wry smile. "Unless he really is a ghost, like the newsmen have been calling him."

They hit the expressway with the warning light flashing, pulled into the far-left lane, and hurtled along in steadily building momentum.

"I don't think there's all this big a hurry, though, Johnny," Weatherbee said uneasily.

"Never can tell," Pappas replied, flicking a gleaming glance toward his superior. "And I sure as hell don't intend to miss this one."

The lieutenant sighed, scratched his cheek again, and said softly: " 'And he gathered them together into a place called in the Hebrew tongue Armageddon.' "

"What?" Pappas said, chancing another quick glance.

"That's from the Book of Revelation," Weatherbee said. "Somehow it seemed appropriate to the moment."

Pappas shivered involuntarily and hunched closer

over the wheel. "Armageddon," he repeated musingly. "That's a sort of hell, isn't it?"

"No," Weatherbee said quietly, hanging onto the door handle to brace himself in the hurtling automobile, "—it's supposed to be the place where the final battle will be fought between the forces of—Christ!—watch it, will you!"

Pappas had swerved between two slower-moving vehicles, setting the lieutenant rocking and swearing beneath his breath.

"Between the forces of what?" he asked, ignoring the complaint.

"Between the forces of good and evil. Goddamnit, we're going to find our Armageddon right here on this expressway if you don't slow this son of a bitch down. Now damnit, that's an order, Johnny!"

Pappas reluctantly released some of the pressure from the accelerator. "Just hurrying to the gathering," he said, grinning. "I sure as hell wouldn't want to miss Armageddon."

"I'll remind you that you said that," Weatherbee said quietly.

6—Execution Hill

The Executioner had left his automobile at a carefully preselected spot in dense brush near the crest of a wooded hill directly opposite the South Hills home of Sergio Frenchi, and was making his fifth trip from the car to his "drop" on the side of the hill. "Execution Hill," as he had come to dub the site, was largely uninhabited, with only three or four residential plots on the entire rise of ground, and there were no buildings of any description on Bolan's side of the hill. Nevertheless he had encountered various sounds of human presence during his trips between car and battlesite, mostly distant rustlings and voices; once he heard a male voice cursing vehemently, and on his third trip a horse and rider crossed his path no more than thirty to forty feet ahead of him, the horse slipping and snorting on the steep hillside and the rider speaking to his mount reassuringly.

The Executioner was exercising the utmost caution and stealth, but there was a lot of equipment to be moved, and he was going ahead with his plans despite the obvious patrol activity around his battlesite. He had selected a shallow hollow lying beneath an outcropping of rock which was angled about thirty degrees easterly of, and roughly ten degrees above, the Frenchi estate, and well-screened behind an overhanging droop of evergreens. He had run his trajectory calculations earlier, based on a range of five hundred yards, estimated. Now he had a GI rangefinder with which to refine those calculations, and he was surprised to learn that his estimate had been so close to reality. He applied the corrections for a 530-yard range, then consulted the graph he'd worked up for the Marlin and decided he would need to target fifteen inches above actual target to allow for trajectory drop. He extended similar calculations for the other weapons he had "commandeered" from the armory earlier, devoted another fifteen minutes to making his "setups," then took time for a leisurely cigarette, carefully shielding the tiny glow from any hostile eyes in the vicinity.

As he smoked, he followed a timeworn tradition and scribbled his thoughts in a black leather-bound book. This concluded, he got to his feet and lightened himself, removing everything from his web belt except the .45 and the knife, even emptying the slit-pockets above his knees of the spare clips for the .45, and moved out quietly in a "recon" of the area.

Weatherbee had told him that The Family was lying in wait for his next assault. This could mean nothing but a planned counterattack, and it would have to be a highly personal and concentrated one if it were to be effective. Bolan was not overly worried about their abilities in this regard, not unless the Mafia army had been recruited from combat-trained veterans of recent warfare. He had blackened his face and even the heavens seemed to be in his corner tonight, a nice broken layer of clouds keeping the night a black one most of the time. He paused beside a tree as one of the occasional breaks in the cloud-cover drifted overhead, briefly illuminating, faintly, Execution Hill. As he waited, stony and hardly breathing, a match flared a few yards uphill from his position and he could hear clearly the heavy exhalation of a cigarette smoke. The heavy darkness descended again almost immediately, and Bolen went into motion with it, moving silently in a tight circle up the hillside, homing in on the glowing tip of the cigarette. He came down from above and to the rear, and to within a matter of feet from the smoker. It was a man alone, his back to Bolan, seated on a rock and hunched slightly forward. Bolan unsheathed his knife, felt on the ground and found a rotted stick, and tossed it over the man's head and a few yards downhill. The stick hit a tree and the man's body stiffened.

"Hank?" he called softly.

Then Bolan was upon him, one arm curled tightly into the throat, the knife moving in a swift arc toward the rib cage. The body went limp, a rifle toppled and slid slowly down into the brush, and Bolan lowered the suddenly still form gently to the ground. He absently crushed out the lighted cigarette which had fallen to the ground, then stepped quietly down the hill, continuing the seek-and-destroy mission.

Mounted police, crashing about on horseback down below, did not particularly trouble his mind, but he could allow no enemy patrols on Execution Hill. His plan for the assault on the stronghold, once the major thrust was underway, would definitely limit his mobility; therefore the area would have to be positively secured before the attack was launched. His finely tuned ears detected another sound off to the right, and he moved toward it through the darkness, himself an item of darkness and silent, sudden death.

The following is an excerpt from The Executioner's diary, headed "Thoughts at Execution Hill."

> I suppose that the chief difference between me and ordinary people is that I recognize the challenges of life and find it impossible to turn my back on them. I can't let somebody else do my killing, or bear my blood-smears, or stand in judgment in my behalf. If there is a battle to be fought, I must fight it. If there is blood to be spilled, I must spill it. If somebody is to be judged, I must stand at the bar. I suppose that I am not truly civilized. Maybe I'm a throwback, to another time, to another kind, to another ideal. But this much I know: I am alive tonight because of violence loose upon the earth.

Each breath I take is paid for by crushed and digested once-living things. Violence is the way of the world because competition is the way of life-perpetuation. Without violence there can be no competition, and without competition there can be no life. Something dies for every instant that something else lives.

I just had the thought that I am being morbid—and why not? Life itself is a morbid business. Each life lived is built upon a hill of death; each body is a living monument to death and a moving graveyard. It is the way of life, and even—no, especially—in a civilization. But in a civilization there are appointed executioners, some appointed to serve the greater good, some the greater evil. I am self-appointed, but this fact in no way alters the responsibilities of office.

Valentina, God love her, would die herself before she would crush the skull of a baby steer—but this tender child thoroughly loves her veal steaks. An executioner of baby steers has been appointed in Valentina's behalf, an executioner to crush the skulls of baby steers and thus provide the juicy steaks for tender Val's table.

Valentina, God protect her, is thoroughly repulsed and disgusted by the evil brought to this earth by men like the *Mafiosi*, yet she would allow every indignity upon herself, even to the final indignity of death, before she would pick up a gun and exterminate the vermin. An executioner of vermin has been appointed in Valentina's behalf—for *all* the Valentinas everywhere. It is a self-appointment, a necessary one in this civilization of ours, and I cannot stand away from the responsibility of this office.

Life is a competition, and I am a competitor. I have the tools and the skills, and I must accept the responsibilities. I will fight the battle, spill the blood, smear myself with it, and stand at the bar of judgment to be crushed and chewed and ingested by those I serve. It is the way of the world. It is the ultimate disposition. Stand ready, *Mafiosi*, The Executioner is here.

7—Battle Order

Sergio Frenchi was a man who loved a good scrap; this much was obvious. The old eyes were sparkling with the excitement of anticipation, and he seemed to infect the others with his enthusiasm. The entire area Family was present, and a roll call would have sounded like a polling of the Greater Chamber of Commerce. Practically every strata of the business and professional communities were represented in the assemblage. There were bankers, lawyers, a medical doctor, accountants, insurance executives, two prominent educators; these rubbing elbows with gambling czars, small-time politicos, and racketeers of every stripe.

It was the first full-council, area-wide, which Leo Turrin had been privileged to attend. He was both amazed and impressed by the number and stature of those present. He moved alongside Nat Plasky and said, "I don't get it. Why bring everybody out at a time like this?"

Sergio himself answered the question, as if on cue, raising his arms to quiet the hubbub. "When The Family is in trouble, The Family belongs together," he intoned. He smiled and let his eyes dance around the large room. "Besides—a lot of you have never had to face up to a real threat before. You're *soft*—look at you, your manicured fingers and your two-dollar cigars—how do you think you got all this *security*, eh? You got it because men like *me*, men who never could relax enough to try those manicures and expensive cigars, were out there *fighting* and *grabbing* while you were in your mama's bellies, *that's* how you got it."

"We're getting an object-lesson," Seymour said, *sotto voce*.

Again right on cue, Sergio continued: "You boys don't know what it feels like to be shot at and—"

"The hell I don't," Plasky growled.

"—maybe it's true what they're saying about the organization, eh? Maybe we get too soft with all this legit business we got going. Don't forget where it all came from! Don't forget those dirty dollars keeping us up there at the front of the line! Listen!" He spread one arm in a dramatic sweep towards a group seated at his right. "I even hear some of The Family is beginning to sneer at boys like these. Leopold, here, and his girl operation. Any of you *gentlemen* got any idea how many millions Leo's operation grossed so far this year? Eh? Well it makes any one of the rest of you look like peanuts! You hear? Peanuts!" He stabbed a shaking finger at a well-dressed man down the table to the left. "You, Scali, where do you think the five million came from to back up your insurance reserves, eh? From heaven?" He waggled the finger and fixed the executive with a stern gaze. "It came from whorehouses, yeah, yeah! How do you good gentlemen think we manage to keep our girls operating, eh? Through our contacts with the Chamber of Commerce? Eh? Lemme tell you all something—*you are soft!* And I—"

"I haven't heard him wind up like this in fifteen years," Seymour whispered.

"I just wish he'd wind down," Turrin said uncomfortably, but his eyes were all attention on the powerful and compelling old warrior at the head of the table. "I'll bet he was a hell of a man in his day," he added softly.

"He survived the wars," Seymour grunted. "He'll survive this one, too. Anybody making book on the outcome?"

"Not a chance," Plasky chimed in softly.

"Now there's guns on the wall down here by the door," Sergio was saying. "Most of you may not get a chance to shoot one off, but you better damn sure have one in your hand when you walk out the door. Don't move around any out in the open, keep yourselves down and don't do anything stupid. We got the regular council room rigged so it looks like we're having a meeting up there. Don't nobody show themselves until he starts banging away, and even then don't do any shooting unless you can see something to shoot at. For God's sake, don't shoot each other. Something else, now, when . . ."

He lectured them for another five minutes, then released them. They straggled out in groups of three and four, a few wise-cracking about the pistols coming down off the wall. Turrin hung back, hoping to get in a few private words with Father Sergio. Plasky and Seymour joined the exiting crowd, Seymour glancing back impatiently at Turrin they going on without him.

Sergio took Turrin by the arm and said, "It's like old times, Leopold. I wish your Uncle Agosto was with us, eh?"

"That'd be great," Turrin agreed, smiling. "I, uh, I been thinking—about that hill across the canyon. We have any men over there?"

The old man was smiling craftily. "No, not on the hill, Leopold. Don't you worry about it. Sergio is ready for the war."

"Well, I was just thinking," Turrin persisted, "—this guy's a soldier, you know. He thinks like a soldier, and I've been thinking . . ."

Sergio patted his arm affectionately. "Don't worry about the soldier," he said grandly. "Sergio has fought a couple of wars himself."

"I'd like to go over there and scout around," Turrin blurted.

"Oh?" The old eyebrows raised in high peaks. "You'd go out there, alone, to meet this in the dark? Eh?"

"Yeah." Turrin shifted uncomfortably under the strong stare. "Regardless of the firepower we have massed over here, he could still slip away from it. I'd like to go over there and plug his escape route."

"What makes you so certain his attack will come from over there?" The tone of voice was plainly teasing.

"I said, he thinks like a soldier. So do I."

The old man laughed, and said, "You're a good soldier, Leopold, and a good *Mafiosi.* Sure, sure, you go over there and take this Bolan single-handed. I believe you can."

Turrin was still not certain if the old man was taunting him or not, but he took the words as official sanction. He left him standing there and raced up the stairs to the main level and ran to the parking lot, extricated his car from the jam, and tore out the drive in full acceleration.

"Where's Leo going?" someone asked, staring after the careening auto.

Sergio stood at the wall, arms crossed over his chest, smiling. "He has gone to beard the lion in his den," he said proudly, then added, under his breath, "I *hope.*"

The speaker crackled and a terse voice announced: "A car is speeding out of the Frenchi estate."

Weatherbee snatched up the mike and said, "Let 'im pass, don't one unit move off station until I give the word!"

"What do you think is going on out there?" Pappas asked.

"Plenty, I'd say," Weatherbee grunted. "I'd give a nickel to get in there and have a look at some of those faces. I bet there'd be some interesting ones."

"Where do you think Bolan will strike from?"

"That's a good question. It's like trying to outguess the quarterback on a third-down play. Tell the truth, I don't envy this Mafia bunch. They have to sit and wait for him to make his hit before they will know how to react and where. It's like waiting for the beginning of an atomic attack, with this Bolan, anyway."

Pappas was grinning. "Well, it's a new role for the Mafia, isn't it. The tables are turned, so to speak."

"Yeah. What time is it?"

"Three-forty."

"See, I told you it would be a damn long night. You want a sandwich?"

Pappas shook his head emphatically. "I couldn't eat a belly dancer's navel right now."

"Nervous?"

"You could say that, yeah. I've been on plenty of stake-outs before, but this one . . ."

"But this one, you're rooting for the other side, is that it?"

Pappas shifted about uncomfortably and lit a cigarette.

"Isn't that it?"

"Well, shit, so what? I kind of admire the guy."

"Don't be embarrassed, Johnny—so do I. I'm just hoping he won't try to shoot his way through a police line, that's all."

"So why do you think I'm butterflies?" Pappas announced, laughing.

"We can't afford to let sentiment ride the trigger finger, Johnny."

"Hell, I know that."

"A sentimental cop is a dead cop."

"Hell, I know that."

"The order is shoot to kill."

"Well, goddamn it, I know that!"

Weatherbee smiled grimly. "Just don't forget it," he said quietly.

8—The Big Kill

The Executioner made a final check of the weaponry and did a mental rehearsal of the sequence of events, then returned to the range finder to study once again the layout on the opposite hillside. For thirty minutes, now, that bunch had been going through the exact same motions, as evidenced by the shadows on the large window. Either they were having a prayer service, or some sort of elaborate rite, or else . . .

He kept his eye to the range finder and moved his watch close alongside and began a timing. *Mark*—the guy at the head of the table lifts an arm at the exact instant the third guy from the end leans over . . . *mark*—three seconds, and somebody walks past in the background . . . *mark*—five seconds, and the arm comes down, the other guy straightens . . . *mark*—three seconds, and a guy walks past in the opposite direction . . . *mark*—five seconds, and . . .

Bolan studied the shadow-movements for a full five minutes, then grinned and moved on to other things. Pretty cute, he had to admit, pretty damn cute—but now, where *really* was the pack congregating? There were very few lights showing. Of this few, all were at the lower levels, with the sole exception of the dim rectangle of light at the large window on level two.

He could make out one corner of the parking lot, and as he watched, a car moved rapidly through the narrow vision-field allowed by the telescopic lens; he followed it, saw the headlamps flare into brilliance, and the car careening along the drive. He wondered about it, but only briefly, returning to the inspection of the house itself. He could see nothing whatever of the roof, no more than a faint outline against the black. He swung back to the ground level, and picked up the figure of a man standing on the patio, near a waist-level wall, partly concealed in shadows. The man moved then, and rubbed something against one shoulder. A pistol—he was scratching his shoulder with the barrel of a pistol. Some idiot. What did they have down there—idiots? The range finder tracked along the wall, seeking other evidence of human habitation. A door flashed open, bright light spilling onto the flagstones for a split second, then was hastily closed. He held the spot and saw the door open again, this time without accompanying light-spillage, and two men scurried out the door and ran up some steps at the corner of the building. Bolan grinned. They were learning—but too slowly. He lost the men in the upper darkness, his wonderment growing with respect to the darkened roof area.

Bolan glanced at his watch, and waited. He had a timed sequence planned, and he preferred a firm jump-off time. Just a few minutes more. He allowed his thoughts to wander to Valentina, to Mom and Pop, to Johnny, the kid he'd barely known and now probably would never know, to Cindy whom he had known better than any living soul and yet had not known at all.

One minute to jump-off. He'd promised Val that he'd be back. An empty promise, one that he'd never expected to keep. Bolan was a soldier—he knew a soldier's odds, he knew the chances of walking off this hillside alive. Cops were all over the place; maybe they'd even bring in dogs. If the Mafia didn't get him, the cops would. Sweet Val. Tender little, passionate little, sweet little Val—a girl who had saved her love only to hand it over to a doomed man. There was a sadness; yes, there was a sadness.

He pushed aside the sadness and moved over to the long tubelike object positioned alongside the range finder, final-checked the azimuth calculations, and began the ten-second countdown. The tube belched and hissed and the projectile roared down the range. The Big Kill was on.

"Jesus Christ!" Pappas yelped. "What was that? Where'd it come from?"

"Rocket of some kind!" Weatherbee yelled.

The streaking glow had roared through the night air at dazzling speed, impacting on the lower corner of the mansion in a thunderous explosion. All lights had winked out and only the dull, licking flames at the devastated corner were providing illumination. A man was screaming in obvious agony, and the excited, raised voices of other men could be heard calling to one another.

Weatherbee and Pappas were on their feet outside the squad car at the perimeter of the property, looking down on the house from about 300 feet. "Where'd the damn thing *come* from?" Pappas repeated excitedly.

"Those hills over there," Weatherbee snapped. "Hand me those binoculars!"

"Think we oughta go down there, maybe give 'em a hand?"

"You outta your mind? They'd shoot us as quick as they'd shoot Bolan. Besides, *he* isn't finished with them, bet your ass on that."

"Good Mary, Mother of God!" Plasky cried. "He's bombing us!"

"Shut up, shut up, and get your head down, you idiot," Seymour snapped. "F'Christ's sake, that was just the first shot!"

"Shot? Shot? You call that a shot? Where's Sergio? What the hell is Sergio doing?"

"Everybody keep down and stay calm," Sergio's voice intoned loudly, floating down from the higher level. "Did anybody see where it came from?"

A chorus of excited voices all tried to report at once.

"Outta the sky!" yelled one.

"Th' south corner!" came another intelligible response.

"It came right outta th' fuckin' moon," reported a voice close to Seymour.

"Aw shit, shit!" Sergio cried. "Keep your eyes open now! Look for a flash, anything, a bit of smoke, just keep your eyes open!"

"Heads up, pip, pip, and all that shit," Seymour muttered to himself.

The Executioner was completing another countdown. He hit *Zero* and the flare gun at the same instant, then smiled and picked up the Marlin, peering through the scope. Seconds later the flare shell opened in the sky directly above the Frenchi mansion and floated gently groundward in startling brilliance, lighting the area like a personal sun. Bolan's scope was already seeking the Frenchi roof when the shell burst into brilliance, a dazed, upturned face raised to the white hot sun loomed into the vision-field and Bolan's educated finger took spontaneous action. The big gun roared and bucked against him; he fought it steady, hanging grimly to the eyepiece and saw his target go down, hands digging at the belly. Bolan nodded in confirmation of his correction; from chin to belly was about 15 inches. He swung slightly left and picked up another target; another squeeze and buck; a few more degrees left, another target, again a squeeze; and another, and another, and he had counted off but five seconds. He laid down the Marlin and bent his eye to the range finder for a broader view. That roof was full of men, some still standing and staring stupidly into the brilliance, others seemingly frozen with surprise and fear, one was trying to support a bloody and obviously dead body; but most were at least partially concealed behind the low parapet at the edge of the roof. Obviously nobody had spotted his muzzle-flashes; there was no return fire.

Bolan shook his head sadly, muttered, "*Who's* the amateur?" and went into another countdown.

"There's four dead and one wounded up here" an excited voice called down.

"Sergio! Sergio? What do we do?"

"How long do those damn things burn?"

"Down, down, everybody keep down and eyes open!" It was Sergio, huffing with excitement. "Pete! Barney! Start raking that hillside!"

The abrupt chatter of a machine gun broke the deadening pall, then another, and nobody really cared if there were a target to shoot at or not. Just the sound of firepower, coming from their camp, was a comfort in itself. Then another light streaked in from the darkness.

"Christ, lookit, another whizzer!"

The rocket slammed into the roof with a heart-stopping thunder of sound and flame, just as the flare burned out, dislodging men, stone, and mortar alike to rain onto the patio below. Screams of terror and groans of agony rose up in its wake, and then there was nothing but the frightening blackness of the night. A machine gun resumed its chatter, firing sporadically, but there was little cheer to its impotent message. Men were running blindly through the darkness. Muffled curses, labored breathing, and exclamations of pain and horror told the story of untrained would-be combatants; and still it was not the ending, but only the beginning. The walking explosions began then, in a pattern of terror that left no stone of the Frenchi mansion untouched or unshaken. And even the machine guns ceased their useless chatter, and the exodus of The Family was in full sway.

"He's shelling them with mortar fire," Weatherbee announced grimly. "My God, that must be sheer hell down there."

"Where'd that guy *get* that kind of stuff?" Pappas wondered, in an awed voice.

"That's not the point. The point is, he knows how to use it. Hell, this is full-scale warfare. One-sided, yeah, but hell, this is the side I was feeling sorry for. Jesus Christ!"

The vibrations of warfare were being felt even from their vantage point, and a chunk of shrapnel whizzed into the door of the squad car, missing Pappas by inches. "Hit-the-fuckin'-dirt," he said calmly, and fell to a prone position alongside the car.

"I think I've spotted him," Weatherbee declared. "Near the top of the hill, almost directly across from the house. You can't see anything from these mortar launchings, but if he shoots another of these rockets—well, just keep your eyes peeled thataway."

The sergeant's eyes were peeled another way, however, onto the horror of sound, vibration, and powder flashes below; then another flare lit up the sky, and the sergeant shielded his eyes from the brilliance and peered dutifully toward the distant hill. "What a guy," he said softly. "What a hell of a guy."

The hell of a guy was having troubling second thoughts of his own. It had gone entirely too easily. The enemy was in full rout and not one threat, not one, had come his way. Either he had grossly overestimated them, or else.... He put his eye to the Marlin's scope and rapid-fired five rounds into an automobile that was swerving along the looping driveway. The car left the drive, curved about, and bounced back onto it and toppled onto its side like a toy, then burst into flames. Another car, which had been following closely behind, plowed into the wreckage, and moments later there was another explosion. The scene revealed beneath the glare of the second flare was a tribute to carnage and destruction. The house was all but levelled, two of its walls standing grotesquely in a pall of dust and smoke. Many of the cars in the parking area were buried beneath debris; broken windows and damaged bodies of others showed the marks of concussion and flying objects. Human bodies were strewn everywhere.

"They should have a big punch somewhere," Bolan murmured. "Surely, surely." He fired off another flare and began searching the rubble through the range finder; then he heard a familiar sound, one he had not heard at such close range since Vietnam; it was a chopper, a helicopter, and it was close, damn close. Cops? he wondered. Or The Family's big punch?

Bolan hastily selected a flare with a short-time fuse, reset the azimuth on the flare gun, and let it fly. It flashed into brilliance almost immediately, lighting the sky at high altitude above the canyon floor and catching the chopper in bright illumination. It was so close that Bolan could see the pilot throw a protecting arm across his eyes, and the startled face of a white-haired man showed clearly in the window. The settling flare also illuminated Bolan's position; the chopper heeled rapidly over into darkness as Bolan reached for the Marlin. He could hear it swooping close in a tight circle, then it edged back into the flare's circle of light and began spitting fire at him from the rear deck as an automatic weapon began unloading on him. The range finder skittered away, propelled by a steel-jacketed slug, and Bolan rolled away, fighting the Marlin to his shoulder, fighting also an impulse to fire from the hip, and then the chopper was gone again. Bolan rolled over to a tree stump and sat placidly, waiting, sighting along the side of the scope toward the sound of the windmill.

Suddenly it was back, heeling in from the other direction, and Bolan's eye slid over onto the eyepiece and his trained finger waited for a target. A white-maned head appeared in the vision-field, clear enough for Bolan to read the bubbling excitement in the heavy-browed eyes, and then his finger did its part, the big gun bucked, and the excitement went out of white-head's eyes as the chatter of the machine gun once again took up the challenge.

"I can see him!" Pappas said excitedly. "They see him too. Hey! They've got a machine gun in that chopper!"

"Gimme those damn glasses!" Weatherbee commanded.

"Here—hell—don't even need glasses! Hell—this is like the TV reports on the Vietnam fighting."

"This ain't Vietnam, kiddo," Weatherbee murmured.

"Hell, who'd know it?"

"That son of a bitch. How about that son of a bitch?"

The heavy *cra-ack* of the Marlin came loud and clear above the other sounds, then the heavier staccato of the machine gun, punctuated thrice more by the Marlin's reply. The *thump-whump* of the whirling blades seemed to take on a different sound and the helicopter lurched and wheeled crazily, plainly visible in the light from the still-high flare.

"Well, Goddamn, I believe he hit 'em," Weatherbee breathed.

"Damn right, that chopper is falling!"

"The Executioner," Weatherbee said flatly, "has come through Armageddon."

The Executioner would not have been so quick to agree with Lieutenant Weatherbee's assessment of the battle. His shoulder wound had reopened and the blood was soaking his left side. He watched the chopper disappear into the trees, waited for the explosion and grunted when it came, then limped back over to his drop and fumbled about for the first-aid box. He'd done something to his ankle during that final skirmish, and now he could hear sounds above him, somewhere in the woods. He hastily folded in a gauze compress over the shoulder wound and limped into the shadow of a tree, leaving the Marlin behind and wishing the damn flare would hurry and burn itself out.

Someone was coming down the hillside, obviously trying to be both quiet and quick, and the twain would never meet, not in these woods. A rock the size of a baseball was dislodged and came bounding down the slope to crash into a tree several feet from where Bolan stood. Moments later Leo Turrin hove into view, panting with exertion and tension, the cords of his neck standing out plainly above the V-necked polo shirt.

"Bolan?" he called softly. "Bolan, are you there?"

Bolan shook his head sorrowfully. "Will you never learn, Leo?" he asked, stepping out from behind the tree, the .45 out and ready.

"God*damn* I'm glad you're all right," Turrin declared fervently. "I came over to tell you about the helicopter, but damnit I couldn't find you."

"Who the hell you trying to kid?" Bolan asked, his tone clearly one of disgusted amazement.

Turrin held his hands straight out in front of his body and carefully sat on the ground. "Shit, I gotta give up cigarettes," he said. "I can hardly breathe."

"You gotta give up more than cigarettes, kid," Bolan told him.

"Can I take off one shoe?"

Bolan's shoulder was beginning to burn maddeningly. "Is that your last request?" he asked impatiently.

"Yeah, yeah, call it my last request. Can I take it off?"

The flare was growing dim and was beginning to disappear over the horizon of trees. Bolan moved closer and dropped to one knee, the .45 held grimly forward. "If you've been trying to delay me into darkness, you can forget it already," he said.

Turrin had the shoe off and was peeling out the insole. He withdrew a small plasticized rectangle and proffered it to Bolan. "Look at this first, will you?" he asked quietly.

Bolan studied the small card in the dying light of the flare, trying to keep one eye on his captive while doing so. Then he chuckled and returned the card. "You know how close you've been to being a *dead* undercover man?" he said.

"Shit, I've said so many prayers I'm about to get religion again," Turrin replied, smiling broadly.

"You not interested in arresting me?" Bolan asked whimsically. His fingers moved to the wound and pressed hard against the compress. The .45 remained steady in the weakening arm.

"I have no jurisdiction on this side of the canyon," Turrin said, still smiling. "God, did you unload on those bastards! Is there anything left for the law?"

"I doubt it," Bolan said. Another thought was forming in his mind. "About my sister, Leo . . ."

"I'm guilty," Turrin said matter-of-factly. "It's part of my cover, of course. God, I feel like hell about those kids, kids like your sister. I tried to make it easy on them —you know—steer them into good dates their first few times out, but—well—I've been a lot of years into this case, Sarge. There *are* more important things than individual haywire kids. I just hope you can understand that."

"I can understand it," Bolan said tightly. "Okay. Get on back up the hill, and give my regards to the missus. Oh—by the way, Leo. These hot flashes I've been getting by way of Weatherbee. They come from you?"

Turrin nodded his head soberly. "And all the time you've been trying to toast my ass off."

"Hell, you should have gotten word to me," Bolan said grudgingly.

"There's just one thing I hold against you, Sarge," Turrin declared, his face going into a deep scowl. "I guess I'll never forgive you for tipping my wife. Now

I'm going to have a worried female on my neck all the time, all the damn time."

"That's the only kind to have," Bolan said softly. He was thinking of another worrier, and he did not like the feel of his own blood trickling down his side. "Get on up the hill now. I have to blow this place."

Turrin slipped the shoe back onto his foot, stood up and tossed Bolan a military salute, and disappeared into the enfolding woods. Bolan grunted and moved painfully down the slope, back to his drop, and retrieved a few personally prized items, made another attempt to staunch the flow of blood from the old wound, then descended slowly to the canyon floor below.

Automobiles were racing around up topside on both sides of the canyon, and Bolan knew that the police were closing in to seal off the area and to pick up the pieces. A horse whinned off to Bolan's right, and with a bravado born of bleeding desperation he called: "Over here. Hey! Over here!"

He stepped into a flowering bush and waited, and a moment later was rewarded by the appearance of a walking man with a horse in tow. Bolan smacked the .45 against the deputy's head and seized the reins, hoisted himself aboard, and headed out across the canyon. Day would be breaking in less than an hour. There wasn't much time to get back home to his worried woman. He knew he wouldn't make it all the way on the horse. All he wanted now was distance, and a little time, and a lot of luck. Maybe he would not be ingested this time, after all. Victory was not sweet for The Executioner. Victory was a burning shoulder and a nauseous gut and an ache in the heart for the tender woman who waited. But, at least, he had not been ingested yet.

9—The Victory

Bolan awoke with a start and gazed up into the deep brown pools of Valentina's eyes.

"Gosh, you always wake up and catch me staring at you," she said lightly.

Bolan blinked. "Have I been dreaming?" he asked weakly. "Or has this all happened before?"

His shoulder was freshly bandaged and he was aware of the sheets against bare skin; he was naked. "Yeah, it's happened before," he said, answering his own question.

Valentina leaned forward and kissed him softly on the lips. "You passed out in the doorway," she told him. "Don't you remember that?"

"I just feel weak, weak, weak," he mumbled.

"Well, you should, and it serves you right," she said. She held up a newspaper which had been draped across her lap. "It says here that you killed twenty-three men last night, and seriously injured another fifty-one."

"It says that?"

"Uh-huh. Can't you see the headline?"

He focused his eyes on the bold black print atop the newspaper. " 'Executioner rubs out Mafia,' " he read aloud, then closed his eyes and stretched an arm to grasp her hand. It felt warm, soft, and tiny—and Bolan's heart lurched. "God, Val, I thought I wouldn't make it," he murmured.

She lay down beside him, carefully arranging herself away from the wound, and placed her face against his. "I would have never forgiven you if you hadn't," she whispered.

"It's going to be okay now," he assured her.

"I know. The war's over, and you've won."

"Not the war, honey, just a battle. You have to understand that. The war is still on. All I've won is a battle."

She stiffened momentarily, then flowed back against him. "While you were sleeping, you kept groaning that there was no victory. What did you mean?"

"I don't know," he replied honestly.

"Well, don't you feel a sense of victory?"

Bolan cautiously positioned his weak arm about her and followed up with a tight clasp of the good one. Of course he felt a sense of victory—but not until this moment, not until right now. "A man fights *for* things—not against things," he said.

She drew back to gaze at him. He opened his eyes and returned the frank stare. "You're deep, you know," she told him. "You are *very* deep. Now just what did you mean by that?"

He smiled, ignoring the pain of his shoulder. "Freely translated," he replied, "it means, tender Val, that I love you *nutty*."

"That's a victory?" she asked, the lights flaring deep in her eyes.

"It's the only victory a man can ever know," he assured her.

She moved away from him, got to her feet slipped off the simple housecoat, her only garment, drew back the sheet, and slid in alongside him, pressing herself in close conjunction. "As soon as you get your strength back," she told him, "I'll challenge you to demonstrate that victory."

"Hell, there's nothing wrong with my strength," he said, grinning. "My strength isn't in my shoulder, silly."

"I know where your strength is," she murmured. "The honeymoon wasn't that short. Anyway, it isn't even over. Is it?"

"Some things, like war and love, are never over," he said, folding her in closer.

"Which is this?" she asked tremulously.

"*This*," he replied, "is *victory* in *both*."

She sighed and lay her face in the hollow of his throat. "Victory is so sweet," she whispered.

EPILOGUE

The battle of Pittsfield had ended. Victory, for Mack Bolan, had been not an era but a miniscule point in time which had already receded into the fuzzy past, one that was absorbed and neutralized by the perilous present and which stood under the constant threat of being reversed by the uncertain future. Bolan had not killed an idea, nor a system; he had barely rippled the surface of the most powerful underworld organization in existence. Already, he knew, the full resources of that organization would be gearing up to flick away the gnat which was gnawing on its shinbone. There were no self-deceptions for Bolan; he knew that he was perhaps the most marked man in underworld history. He had, overnight, become an American legend; a plum to be picked by every ambitious law enforcer in the nation; sudden riches to be cashed in by every two-bit punk with a gun in the country; a debt to be settled by each member of the far-flung family of Mafia around the world.

Mack Bolan was marked for death; he realized that he was as condemned as any man who had ever sat on death row. His chief determination was to stretch that last mile to its highest yield, to fight the war to its last gasp, to "eat their bowels even as they are trying to digest me."

Bolan had taken steps to minimize his personal danger. He had changed the color of his hair, grown a moustache, and adopted horn-rimmed, clear-lens glasses. This cover, he hoped, would at least see him safely to the West Coast. A better cover awaited him there, in the talents of a former Army surgeon who owed his life to Mack Bolan—a surgeon whose battlefield experiences had given rise to his present specialty: cosmetic surgery. Bolan would find a new face on the West Coast. He left behind, in Pittsfield, an orphaned brother, a chunk of money, and a pretty girl to administer both. He left behind, also, an identity; one which perhaps he would never again to able to claim.

Bolan swung his newly acquired vehicle onto the west expressway of Pittsfield on the evening of September 12th, blending in with the rush-hour traffic, Val's tearful goodbye still influencing his emotions. Behind lay everything he had ever held dear. Ahead lay everything he had ever learned to fear. He cleared his mind of self-pity, letting go even of the image of tender Val, and scowled into the bright glow of the setting sun. There was nothing ahead but hell. He was prepared for hell. Somebody else, he avowed, had better get prepared for it, too. Mack Bolan's last mile would be a bloody one. The Executioner was going to live life to the very end.